Anonymous

Rhymes and Roundelayes in Praise of a Country Life

Anonymous

Rhymes and Roundelayes in Praise of a Country Life

ISBN/EAN: 9783337192167

Printed in Europe, USA, Canada, Australia, Japan

Cover: Foto ©Andreas Hilbeck / pixelio.de

More available books at **www.hansebooks.com**

RHYMES AND ROUNDELAYES

IN PRAISE OF A

COUNTRY LIFE.

ILLUSTRATED BY BIRKET FOSTER, HARRISON WEIR,
AND OTHER ARTISTS.

London and New York:

GEORGE ROUTLEDGE AND SONS,

1875.

" Colin, to heare thy rymes and roundelayes,
Which thou wert wont on wastefull hilles to sing,
I more delight than lark in sommer dayes
Whose eccho made the neighbour groves to ring."—SPENSER.

LONDON:
R. CLAY, SONS, AND TAYLOR, PRINTERS.
BREAD STREET HILL.

CONTENTS

CONTENTS.

LIST OF ILLUSTRATIONS

LIST OF ILLUSTRATIONS.

The Ornamental Initial Letters drawn by THOMAS MACQUOID.
The Tail-pieces by JANE E. HAY.

MAY MORNING.

Now the bright morning star, day's harbinger,
Comes dancing from the East, and leads with her
The flow'ry May, who from her green lap throws
The yellow cowslip and the pale primrose.
 Hail, bounteous May ! that dost inspire
 Mirth, and youth, and warm desire :
 Woods and groves are of thy dressing,
 Hill and dale doth boast thy blessing.
Thus we salute thee with our early song,
And welcome thee and wish thee long.

MILTON.

And more magnificent art thou, bright Sun!
U'prising from the Ocean's billowy bed

THE SUN.

OST glorious art thou! when from thy pavilion
    Thou lookest forth at morning; flinging wide
Its curtain clouds of purple and vermilion,
    Dispensing life and light on every side;
Brightening the mountain cataract, dimly spied
    Through glittering mist; opening each dew-gemm'd
        flower,
Or touching, in some hamlet, far descried,
    Its spiral wreaths of smoke that upward tower,
While birds their matins sing from many a leafy bower.

3

And more magnificent art thou, bright Sun !
Uprising from the Ocean's billowy bed :
Who that has seen thee thus, as I have done,
Can e'er forget the effulgent splendours spread
From thy emerging radiance ?   Upwards sped,
Even to the centre of the vaulted sky,
Thy beams pervade the heavens, and o'er them shed
Hues indescribable—of gorgeous dye,
Making among the clouds mute glorious pageantry.

Then, then how beautiful across the deep
The lustre of thy orient path of light !
Onward, still onward, o'er the waves that leap
So lovelily, and show their crests of white,
The eye, unsated in its own despite,
Still up that vista gazes ; till thy way
Over the waters seems a pathway bright
For holiest thoughts to travel, there to pay
Man's homage unto Him who bade thee "rule the Day."

Barton.

UP, AMARYLLIS!

AKEN, thou fair one ! up, Amaryllis !
   Morning so still is ;
   Cool is the gale :
   The rainbow of heaven,
   With its hues seven,
   Brightness hath given
   To wood and dale.
Sweet Amaryllis, let me convey thee ;
In Neptune's arms nought shall affray thee ;
Sleep's god no longer power has to stay thee,
Over thy eyes and speech to prevail.

4

Come out a-fishing; nets forth are carrying.
 Come without tarrying—
 Hasten with me.
 Jerkin and vail in—
 Come for the sailing,
 For trout and grayling :
 Baits will lay we.
Awake, Amaryllis ! dearest, awaken ;
Let me not go forth by thee forsaken ;
Our course among dolphins and sirens taken,
Onward shall paddle our boat to the sea.

Bring rod and line—bring nets for the landing ;
 Morn is expanding,
 Hasten away !
 Sweet ! no denying,
 Frowning, or sighing—
 Couldst thou be trying
 To answer me Nay?
Hence, on the shallows, our little boat leaving,
Or to the Sound, where green waves are heaving,
Where our true love its first bond was weaving,
Causing to Thirsis so much dismay.

Step in the boat, then ! both of us singing.
 Love afresh springing,
 O'er us shall reign.
 If the storm rages,
 If it war wages,
 Thy love assuages
 Terror and pain.
Calm 'mid the billows' wildest commotion,
I would defy on thy bosom the ocean,
Or would attend thee to death with devotion :
Sing, O ye sirens, and mimic my strain !—*Bellman.*

MORNING.

ISH'D morning 's come ; and now upon
the plains
And distant mountains, where they feed
their flocks,
The happy shepherds leave their homely huts,
And with their pipes proclaim the new-born day !
The lusty swain comes with his well-fill'd stoup
Of healthful viands, which, when hunger calls,
With much content and appetite he eats,
To follow in the field his daily toil,
And dress the grateful glebe that yields him fruits.
The beasts, that under the warm hedges slept,
And weather'd out the cold, bleak night, are up,
And, looking toward the neighbouring pastures, raise
Their voice, and bid their fellow-brutes good-morrow !
The cheerful birds, too, on the tops of trees,
Assemble all in choirs, and with their notes
Salute and welcome up the rising sun.

Otway.

MORNING MELODIES.

BUT who the melodies of morn can tell?
  The wild brook babbling down the mountain side;
The lowing herd, the sheepfold's simple bell;
  The pipe of early shepherd dim descried

In the lone valley; echoing far and wide
The clamorous horn along the cliffs above;
The hollow murmur of the ocean tide;
The hum of bees, the linnet's lay of love,
And the full choir that wakes the universal grove.

The cottage curs at early pilgrim bark;
Crown'd with her pail, the tripping milkmaid sings;
The whistling ploughman stalks afield; and, hark!
Down the rough slope the ponderous waggon rings;
Through rustling corn the hare, astonish'd, springs;
Slow tolls the village clock the drowsy hour—
The partridge bursts away on whirring wings;
Deep mourns the turtle in sequester'd bower,
And shrill lark carols clear from her aërial tour.

Beattie.

MORNING WALK.

HE morning hath not lost her virgin blush,
Nor step, but mine, soil'd the earth's tinsell'd robe.
How full of heaven this solitude appears—
This healthful comfort of the happy swain,
Who from his hard but peaceful bed roused up,
In morning's exercise saluted is
By a full choir of feather'd choristers,
Wedding their notes to the enamour'd air!
There Nature, in her unaffected dress,
Plaited with valleys, and emboss'd with hills,
Enlaced with silver streams, and fringed with woods,
Sits lovely in her native russet.

Chamberlayne.

8

A SUMMER MORNING.

AND soon, observant of approaching day,
The meek-eyed Morn appears, mother of
dews,
At first faint gleaming in the dappled east ;
Till far o'er ether spreads the widening
glow,
And from before the lustre of her face
White break the clouds away.   With
quicken'd step,
Brown Night retires : young Day pours
in apace,
And opens all the lawny prospect wide.
The dripping rock, the mountain's misty
top,
Swell on the sight, and brighten with the dawn.
Blue, through the dusk, the smoking currents shine ;
And from the bladed field the fearful hare
Limps, awkward : while along the forest glade
The wild deer trip, and, often turning, gaze
At early passenger.   Music awakes
The native voice of undissembled joy ;
And thick around the woodland hymns arise.
Roused by the cock, the soon-clad shepherd leaves
His mossy cottage, where with Peace he dwells ;
And from the crowded fold, in order, drives
His flock, to taste the verdure of the morn.
But yonder comes the powerful King of Day,
Rejoicing in the east !   The lessening cloud,
The kindling azure, and the mountain's brow,
Illumed with fluid gold, his near approach

9   c

Betoken glad. Lo ! now, apparent all,
Aslant the dew-bright earth and colour'd air,
He looks in boundless majesty abroad ;
And sheds the shining day, that burnish'd plays
On rocks, and hills, and towers, and wandering streams,
High-gleaming from afar.

Thomson.

MORNING.

T' was a lovely Morning;—all was calm,
As if Creation, thankful for repose,
In renovated beauty, breathing balm
And blessedness around, from slumber
rose ;
Joyful once more to see the East unclose
Its gates of glory :—yet subdued and
mild,
Like the soft smile of Patience, amid woes
By Hope and Resignation reconciled,
That Morning's beauty shone, that landscape's charm
beguiled.

The heavens were mark'd by many a filmy streak,
Even in the orient ; and the Sun shone through
Those lines, as Hope upon a mourner's cheek
Sheds, meekly chasten'd, her delightful hue.
From groves and meadows, all empearl'd with dew,
Rose silvery mists,—no eddying wind swept by,—
The cottage chimneys, half conceal'd from view
By their embowering foliage, sent on high
Their pallid wreaths of smoke, unruffled to the sky.

And every gentle sound which broke the hush
Of Morning's still serenity, was sweet :
The sky-lark overhead ; the speckled thrush,
Who now had taken with delight his seat
Upon the slender larch, the day to greet ;
The starling, chattering to her callow young ;
And that monotonous lay, which seems to fleet
Like echo through the air, the cuckoo's song,
Was heard at times far off the leafy woods among.

Barton.

MORNING.

WIFTLY from the mountain's brow,
   Shadows, nursed by Night, retire ;
And the peeping sunbeam now
   Paints with gold the village spire.

Philomel forsakes the thorn,
   Plaintive where she prates at night ;
And the lark, to meet the Morn,
   Soars beyond the shepherd's sight.

From the low-roof'd cottage ridge,
   See the chattering swallow spring ;
Darting through the one-arch'd bridge,
   Quick she dips her dappled wing.

Now the pine-tree's waving top
   Gently greets the Morning gale :
Kidlings now begin to crop
   Daisies in the dewy dale.

11

From the balmy sweets, uncloy'd,
(Restless till her task be done,)

Now the busy bee's employ'd
Sipping dew before the sun.

Trickling through the creviced rock,
  Where the limpid stream distils,
Sweet refreshment waits the flock
  When 'tis sun-drove from the hills.

Colin, for the promised corn
  (Ere the harvest hopes are ripe)
Anxious, hears the huntman's horn,
  Boldly sounding, drown his pipe.

Sweet, O sweet, the warbling throng,
  On the white emblossom'd spray !
Nature's universal song
    Echoes to the rising day.

Cunningham.

SPRING.

ALAS, delicious Spring! God sends thee down
To breathe upon his cold and perish'd works
Beauteous revival; earth should welcome thee—
Thee and the west wind, thy smooth paramour,
With the soft laughter of her flowery meads,
Her joys, her melodies: the prancing stag
Flutters the shivering fern; the steed shakes out
His main, the dewy herbage, silver-webb'd,
With frank step trampling; the wild goat looks down
From his empurpling bed of heath, where break
The waters deep and blue, with crystal gleams
Of their quick-leaping people; the fresh lark

14

Is in the morning sky ; the nightingale
Tunes evensong to the dropping waterfall.
Creation lives with loveliness—all melts
And trembles into one wild harmony.

Milman.

SPRING.

BEHOLD the young, the rosy Spring
Gives to the breeze her scented wing,
While virgin graces, warm with May,
Fling roses o'er her dewy way.
The murmuring billows of the deep
Have languish'd into silent sleep.
And mark ! the flitting sea-birds lave
Their plumes in the reflecting wave ;
While cranes from hoary winter fly
To flutter in a kinder sky.
Now the genial star of day
Dissolves the murky clouds away,
And cultured field and winding stream
Are freshly glittering in his beam.
Now the earth prolific swells
With leafy buds and flow'ry bells ;
Gemming shoots the olive twine,
Clusters bright festoon the vine ;
All along the branches creeping,
Through the velvet foliage peeping,
Little infant fruits we see
Nursing into luxury.

Moore.

THE RETURN OF SPRING.

USH'D is the howl of wintry breezes wild ;
The purple hour of youthful spring has smiled :
A livelier verdure clothes the teeming earth ;
Buds press to life, rejoicing in their birth ;
The laughing meadows drink the dews of night,
And fresh with opening roses glad the sight :
In song the joyous swains responsive vie ;
Wild music floats and mountain melody.
    Adventurous seamen spread the embosom'd sail
    O'er waves light heaving to the western gale ;
While village youths their brows with ivy twine,
And hail with song the promise of the vine.
    In curious cells the bees digest their spoil,
When vernal sunshine animates their toil,
And little birds, in warblings sweet and clear,
Salute thee, Maia, loveliest of the year :
Thee, on their deeps, the tuneful halcyons hail,
In streams the swan, in woods the nightingale.
    If earth rejoices with new verdure gay,
And shepherds pipe, and flocks exulting play,
And sailors roam, and Bacchus leads his throng,
And bees to toil, and birds awake to song,
Shall the glad bard be mute in tuneful spring,
And, warm with love and joy, forget to sing ?

Bland.

SPRING.

LOOK all around thee!   How the spring advances!
New life is playing through the gay green trees;
See how, in yonder bower, the light leaf dances
To the bird's tread, and to the quivering breeze!

How every blossom in the sunlight glances !
    The winter frost to his dark cavern flees,
And earth, warm-waken'd, feels through every vein
The kindly influence of the vernal rain.
Now silvery streamlets, from the mountains stealing,
    Dance joyously the verdant vales along ;
Cold fear no more the songster's voice is sealing ;
    Down in the thick dark grove is heard his song ;
And, all their bright and lovely hues revealing,
    A thousand plants the field and forest throng ;
Light comes upon the earth in radiant showers,
And mingling rainbows play among the flowers.

Tieck.

SONNET ON SPRING.

NOW Time throws off his cloak again
    Of ermined frost, and cold, and rain,
    And clothes him in the embroidery
    Of glittering sun and clear blue sky.
    With beast and bird the forest rings,
    Each in his jargon cries or sings ;
    And Time throws off his cloak again
    Of ermined frost, and cold, and rain.
River and fount, and tinkling brook,
    Wear in their dainty livery
    Drops of silver jewellery ;
In new-made suit they merry look ;
And Time throws off his cloak again
Of ermined frost, and cold, and rain.

Duke of Orleans.

ODE TO SPRING.

WEET daughter of a rough and stormy sire,
Hoar Winter's blooming child—delightful Spring,
    Whose unshorn locks with leaves
    And swelling buds are crown'd ;

From the green islands of eternal youth,
Crown'd with fresh blooms and ever-springing
      shade,
    Turn, thither turn thy step,
    O thou whose powerful voice,

More sweet than softest touch of Doric reed
Or Lydian flute, can soothe the madding wind,
    And through the stormy deep
    Breathe thine own tender calm. ·

Thee, best beloved ! the virgin train await
With songs, and festal rites, and joy to rove
    Thy blooming wilds among,
    And vales and dewy lawns,

With untired feet ; and cull thy earliest sweets
To weave fresh garlands for the glowing brow
    Of him, the favour'd youth,
    That prompts their whisper'd sigh.

Unlock thy copious stores—those tender showers
That drop their sweetness on the infant buds ;
    And silent dews that swell
    The milky ear's green stem,

And feed the flowering osier's early shoots ;
And call those winds which through the whispering boughs
      With warm and pleasant breath
      Salute the blowing flowers.

Now let me sit beneath the whitening thorn,
And mark thy spreading tints steal o'er the dale ;
      And watch with patient eye
      Thy fair, unfolding charms.

O nymph, approach ! while yet the temperate sun
With bashful forehead through the cold, moist air,
      Throws his young maiden beams,
      And with chaste kisses woos

The earth's fair bosom ; while the streaming veil
Of lucid clouds, with kind and frequent shade,
      Protects thy modest blooms
      From his severer blaze.

Sweet is thy reign, but short ; the red dog-star
Shall scorch thy tresses ; and the mower's scythe
      Thy greens, thy flowerets all,
      Remorseless shall destroy.

Reluctant shall I bid thee then farewell ;
For oh, not all that Autumn's lap contains
      Nor Summer's ruddiest fruits
      Can aught for thee atone,

Fair Spring ! whose simplest promise more delights
Than all their largest wealth, and through the heart
      Each joy and new-born hope
      With softest influence breathes.

                      Barbauld.

MAY.

MAY, sweet May, again is come—
May that frees the land from gloom ;
Children, children, up and see
All her stores of jollity !

On the laughing hedgerow's side
She hath spread her treasures wide ;
She is in the greenwood shade,
Where the nightingale hath made
Every branch and every tree
Ring with her sweet melody ;
Hill and dale are May's own treasures.
Youths, rejoice ! In sportive measures
  Sing ye ! join the chorus gay !
  Hail this merry, merry May !

Up, then, children ! we will go
Where the blooming roses grow ;
In a joyful company
We the bursting flowers will see :
Up ; your festal dress prepare !
Where gay hearts are meeting—there
May hath pleasures most inviting,
Heart, and sight, and ear delighting.
Listen to the bird's sweet song ;
Hark ! how soft it floats along ;
Courtly dames our pleasures share !
Never saw I a May so fair ;
Therefore dancing will we go.
Youths, rejoice ! the flowerets blow !
  Sing ye ! join the chorus gay !
  Hail this merry, merry May !

Our manly youths, where are they now ?
Bid them up and with us go,
To the sporters on the plain :
Bid adieu to care and pain.
Now, thou pale and wounded lover !
Thou thy peace shalt soon recover,

Many a laughing lip and eye
Speaks the light heart's gaiety ;
Lovely flowers around we find,
In the smiling verdure twined ;
Richly steep'd in May-dews glowing.
Youths, rejoice ! the flowers are blowing !
   Sing ye ! join the chorus gay !
   Hail this merry, merry May !

Oh, if to my love restored—
To her, o'er all her sex adored—
What supreme delight were mine !
How would care her sway resign ?
Merrily in the bloom of May
Would I weave a garland gay.
Better than the best is she,
Purer than all purity ;
For her spotless self alone,
I will praise this changeless one :
Thankful, or unthankful, she
Shall my song, my idol be.
   Youths, then join the chorus gay !
   Hail this merry, merry May !

Kirchberg.

SPRING.

YOUNG folk now flock in everywhere,
To gather May-bushes and smelling brere.
And home they hasten the posts to dight,
And all the kirk pillars, ere daylight,
With hawthorn-buds, and sweet eglantine,
And garlands of roses.———
Even this morning—no longer ago—
I saw a shoal of shepherds outgo,
With singing, and shouting, and jolly cheer:
Before them went a lusty tabourer,
That unto many a hornpipe play'd,
Whereto they danced, each one with his maid.
To see these folk making such joyance
Made my heart after the pipe to dance.
Then to the greenwood they speed them all
To fetch home May, with their musical:
And home they bring him, in a royal throne,
Crown'd as king; and his queen—fair one—
Was Lady Flora, on whom did attend
A fair flock of fairies, and a fresh bend
Of lovely nymphs.   Oh that I were there,
To help the ladies their May-bush to bear!

Spenser.

SPRING.

THE snow has left the cottage-top ;
   The thatch-moss grows in brighter green ;
And eaves in quick succession drop,
   Where grinning icicles have been,
Pit-patting with a pleasant noise
   In tubs set by the cottage-door :

While ducks and geese, with happy joys,
  Plunge in the yard-pond brimming o'er.

The sun peeps through the window-pane,
  Which children mark with laughing eye,
And in the wet streets steal again,
  To tell each other Spring is nigh.
Then as young Hope the past recalls,
  In playing groups they often draw,
To build beside the sunny walls
  Their spring-time huts of sticks or straw.

And oft in pleasure's dream they hie
  Round homesteads by the village side,
Scratching the hedge-row mosses by,
  Where painted pooty shells abide ;
Mistaking oft the ivy spray
  For leaves that come with budding spring,
And wondering, in their search for play,
  Why birds delay to build and sing.

The mavis thrush, with wild delight,
  Upon the orchard's dripping tree
Mutters, to see the day so bright,
  Fragments of young Hope's poesy ;
And Dame oft stops her buzzing wheel,
  To hear the robin's note once more,
Who tootles while he pecks his meal
  From sweet-briar hips beside the door.

Clare.

THE AWAKENING YEAR.

HE blue-birds and the violets
   Are with us once again,
And promises of summer spot
   The hill-side and the plain.

The clouds along the mountain-tops
   Are riding on the breeze,
Their trailing azure trains of mist
   Are tangled in the trees.

The snow-drifts, which have lain so long
   Haunting the hidden nooks,
Like guilty ghosts have slipp'd away,
   Unseen, into the brooks.

The streams are fed with generous rain,
   They drink the wayside springs,
And flutter down from crag to crag,
   Upon their foamy wings.

Through all the long wet nights they brawl,
   By mountain-homes remote,
Till woodmen in their sleep behold
   Their ample rafts afloat.

The lazy wheel that hung so dry
　Above the idle stream,
Whirls wildly in the misty dark,
　And through the miller's dream.

Loud torrent unto torrent calls,
　Till at the mountain's feet,
Flashing afar their spectral light,
　The noisy waters meet.

They meet, and through the lowlands sweep,
　Toward briny bay and lake,
Proclaiming to the distant towns
　" The country is awake ! "

Reed.

SONG.

U P, up ! let us greet
The season so sweet,
　For winter is gone,
And the flowers are springing,
And little birds singing,
Their soft notes ringing,
　And bright is the sun !
Where all was dress'd
In a snowy vest ;
Their grass is growing,
With dew-drops glowing,
　And flowers are seen
　On beds of green.
All down in the grove,
Around, above,
　Sweet music floats ;

28

As now loudly vying,
Now softly sighing,
The nightingale 's plying
  Her tuneful notes ;
And joyous at spring
Her companions sing.
Up, maidens, repair
To the meadows so fair,
  And dance we away,
  This merry May.

Von Nifen.

DESCRIPTION OF SPRING.

HE soote season, that bud and bloom
    forth brings,
  With green hath clad the hill, and eke
    the vale ;
  The nightingale with feathers new she
    sings ;
    The turtle to her mate hath told her tale.
  Summer is come, for every spray now springs ;
    The hart hath hung his old head on the
      pale,
The buck in brake his winter coat he flings ;
  The fishes flete with new repaired scale ;
The adder all her slough away she flings ;
  The swift swallow pursueth the flies smale ;
The busy bee her honey now she mings ;
  Winter is worn that was the flowers' bale.
And thus I see among these pleasant things
Each care decays, and yet my sorrow springs.

Surrey.

ON SPRING.

SWEET Spring, thou com'st with all thy goodly train,
 Thy head with flames, thy mantle bright with flow'rs,
 The zephyrs curl the green locks of the plain,
 The clouds for joy in pearls weep down their show'rs.
 Sweet Spring, thou com'st—but, ah ! my pleasant hours
 And happy days with thee come not again ;
 The sad memorials only of my pain
 Do with thee come, which turns my sweets to sours.
Thou art the same which still thou wert before,—
Delicious, lusty, amiable, fair ;
But she whose breath embalm'd thy wholesome air
Is gone ; nor gold, nor gems, can her restore.
 Neglected virtues, seasons go and come,
 When thine forgot lie closed in a tomb.
What doth it serve to see the sun's bright face,
And skies enamell'd with the Indian gold ?
Or the moon in a fierce chariot roll'd,
And all the glory of that starry place ?
What doth it serve earth's beauty to behold,
The mountain's pride, the meadow's flow'ry grace,
The stately comeliness of forests old,
The sport of floods which would themselves embrace ?
What doth it serve to hear the sylvans' songs,
The cheerful thrush, the nightingale's sad strains,
Which in dark shades seem to deplore my wrongs ?
For what doth serve all that this world contains,
 Since she for whom those once to me were dear,
 Can have no part of them now with me here ?

Drummond.

30

Songs of the Birds.

SONNET.

O NIGHTINGALE, that on yon bloomy spray
  Warblest at eve, when all the woods are still ;
  Thou with fresh hope the lover's heart dost fill,
While the jolly hours lead on propitious May.
Thy liquid notes, that close the eve of day,
  First heard before the shallow cuckoo's bill,
  Portend success in love ; oh ! if Jove's will
Have link'd that amorous power to thy soft lay,
  Now timely sing, ere the rude bird of hate
Foretell my hopeless doom in some grove nigh.
  As thou from year to year hast sung too late
For my relief, yet hadst no reason why :
  Whether the muse or love call thee his mate,
Both them I serve, and of their train am I. *Milton.*

31

THE LARK.

IRD of the wilderness,
　　Blithesome and cumberless,
Sweet be thy matins o'er moorland and lea !
　　Emblem of happiness,
　　Blest is thy dwelling-place—
Oh to abide in the desert with thee !
　　Wild is thy lay, and loud,
　　Far in the downy cloud ;
Love gives it energy—love gave it birth :
　　Where, on thy dewy wing—
　　Where art thou journeying ?
Thy lay is in heaven—thy love is on earth.

　　O'er fell and fountain sheen,
　　O'er moor and mountain green,
O'er the red streamer that heralds the day,
　　Over the cloudlet dim,
　　Over the rainbow's rim,
Musical cherub, soar, singing, away !
　　Then, when the gloaming comes,
　　Low in the heather blooms,
Sweet will thy welcome and bed of love be !
　　Emblem of happiness,
　　Blest is thy dwelling-place—
Oh to abide in the desert with thee !

Hogg.

THE WATER-WAGTAIL

OH, the sunny summer time!
   Oh, the leafy summer time!
Merry is the bird's life,
   When the year is in its prime!

Birds are by the waterfalls
    Dashing in the rainbow-spray ;
Everywhere, everywhere
    Light and lovely there are they !
Birds are in the forest old,
    Building in each hoary tree ;
Birds are on the green hills ;
    Birds are by the sea !

On the moor, and in the fen,
    'Mong the wortle-berries green ;
In the yellow furze-bush
    There the joyous bird is seen.
In the heather on the hill ;
    All among the mountain thyme ;
By the little brook-sides,
    Where the sparkling waters chime ;
In the crag ; and on the peak,
    Splinter'd, savage, wild, and bare,
There the bird with wild wing
    Wheeleth through the air.

                            Howitt.

THE LARK.

HARK ! hark ! the lark at heaven's gate sings,
    And Phœbus 'gins arise—
His steeds to water at those springs,
    On chaliced flowers that lies ;
And winking Mary-buds begin
    To ope their golden eyes ;
With everything that pretty bin—
    My lady sweet, arise !

                            Shakspeare.

34

THE NIGHTINGALE.

O cloud, no relic of the sunken day,
Distinguishes the west ; no long, thin slip
Of sullen light—no obscure, trembling hues.
Come ; we will rest on this old mossy bridge !
You see the glimmer of the stream beneath,
But hear no murmuring; it flows silently
O'er its soft bed of verdure.   All is still—
A balmy night ! and though the stars be dim,
Yet let us think upon the vernal showers
That gladden the green earth, and we shall find
A pleasure in the dimness of the stars.
And hark ! the nightingale begins its song,
" Most musical, most melancholy " bird !
A melancholy bird ! Oh, idle thought !
In nature there is nothing melancholy.
  *   *   *   'Tis the merry nightingale
That crowds, and hurries, and precipitates
With fast, thick warble his delicious notes,
As he were fearful that an April night
Would be too short for him to utter forth
His lone chant, and disburden his full soul
Of all its music !
              I know a grove
Of large extent, hard by a castle huge,
Which the great lord inhabits not ; and so
This grove is wild with tangling underwood,
And the trim walks are broken up, and grass —
Thin grass—and king-cups grow within the paths.
But never elsewhere in one place I knew

35

So many nightingales ; and far and near,
In wood and thicket, over the wide grove
They answer, and provoke each other's song
With skirmish and capricious passagings,
And murmurs musical, and swift jug-jug,
And one low, piping sound, more sweet than all,
Stirring the air with such a harmony,
That should you close your eyes, you might almost
Forget it was not day !   On moonlit bushes,
Whose dewy leaflets are but half disclosed,
You may, perchance, behold them on the twigs,
Their bright, bright eyes—their eyes both bright and full,
Glistening, while many a glow-worm in the shade
Lights up her love-torch.
          A most gentle maid,
Who dwelleth in her hospitable home,
Hard by the castle, and at latest eve
(Even like a lady vow'd and dedicate
To something more than Nature in the grove),
Glides through the pathways ; she knows all their notes,
That gentle maid ! and oft a moment's space,
What time the moon was lost behind a cloud,
Hath heard a pause of silence ; till the moon
Emerging, hath awaken'd earth and sky
With one sensation, and these wakeful birds
Have all burst forth in choral minstrelsy,
As if some sudden gale had swept at once
A hundred airy harps ! and she hath watch'd
Many a nightingale pitch'd giddily
On blossoming twig still swinging from the breeze,
And to that motion tune his wanton song,
Like tipsy joy that reels with tossing head.
                           Coleridge.

THE THRUSH.

ITHIN a thick and spreading hawthorn bush
　　That overhung a molehill large and round,
I heard, from morn to morn, a merry Thrush
　　Sing hymns to sunrise, while I drank the sound,
With joy :—and often, an intruding guest,
　　I watch'd her secret toils, from day to day,
How true she warp'd the moss to form her nest,
　　And modell'd it within with wood and clay.
And by and by, like heath-bells gilt with dew,
　　There lay her shining eggs as bright as flowers,
Ink-spotted-over shells of green and blue ;
And there I witness'd, in the Summer hours,
A brood of Nature's minstrels chirp and fly,
Glad as the sunshine and the laughing sky.

Clare.

THE NIGHTINGALE.

SWEET Bird, that sing'st away the early hours
　　Of winters past or coming—void of care,
　　Well pleased with delights which present are ;
Fair seasons, budding sprays, sweet-smelling flowers ;
To rocks, to springs, to rills, from leafy bowers,
　　Thou thy Creator's goodness dost declare,
　　And what dear gifts on thee He did not spare ;
A stain to human sense in sin that lowers.
What soul can be so sick, which by thy songs,
　　Attired in sweetness, sweetly is not driven
Quite to forget earth's turmoils, spites and wrongs,
　　And lift a reverent eye and thought to heaven ?

Drummond.

37

NEST OF THE NIGHTINGALE.

UP this green woodland side let's softly rove,
And list the nightingale ; she dwells just here.
Hush ! let the wood-gate softly clap, for fear
The noise might drive her from her home of love ;
For here I've heard her many a merry year—
At morn, at eve—nay, all the live-long day,
As though she lived on song. This very spot,
Just where the old-man's-beard all wildly trails
Rude arbours o'er the road, and stops the way ;
And where the child its blue-bell flowers hath got,
Laughing and creeping through the mossy rails ;
There have I hunted like a very boy,
Creeping on hands and knees through matted thorn,
To find her nest, and see her feed her young,
And vainly did I many hours employ :
All seem'd as hidden as a thought unborn ;
And where those crumpling fern-leaves ramp among
The hazel's under-boughs, I've nestled down
And watch'd her while she sang ; and her renown
Hath made me marvel that so famed a bird
Should have no better dress than russet brown.
Her wings would tremble in her ecstasy,
And feathers stand on end, as 'twere with joy ;
And mouth wide open to release her heart
Of its out-sobbing songs. The happiest part
Of summer's fame she shared, for so to me
Did happy fancy shapen her employ.
But if I touch'd a bush, or scarcely stirr'd,
All in a moment stopt. I watch'd in vain :
The timid bird had left the hazel-bush,

And oft in distance hid to sing again,
Lost in a wilderness of listening leaves,

Rich ecstasy would pour its luscious strain,
Till envy spurr'd the emulating thrush

To start less wild and scarce inferior songs ;
For while of half the year care him bereaves,
To damp the ardour of his speckled breast,
The nightingale to summer's life belongs,
And naked trees, and winter's nipping wrongs
Are strangers to her music, and her rest.
Her joys are ever green—her world is wide !
Hark ! there she is, as usual ; let's be hush ;
For in this black-thorn clump, if rightly guessed,
Her curious house is hidden.   Part aside
Those hazel-branches in a gentle way,
And stoop right cautious 'neath the rustling boughs,
For we will have another search to-day,
And hunt this fern-strewn thorn-clump round and round ;
And where this reeded wood-grass idly bows,
We'll wade right through ; it is a likely nook.
In such like spots, and often on the ground
They'll build, where rude boys never think to look.
Ay ! as I live ! her secret nest is here,
Upon this white-thorn stump !   * * *
We will not plunder music of its dower,
Nor turn this spot of happiness to thrall,
For melody seems hid in every flower
That blossoms near thy home.   These blue-bells all
Seem bowing with the beautiful in song ;
And gaping cuckoo-flower, with spotted leaves,
Seems blushing of the singing it has heard.
How curious is the nest !   No other bird
Uses such loose materials, or weaves
Its dwelling in such spots !   Dead oaken leaves
Are placed without, and velvet moss within ;
And little scraps of grass, and scant and spare,
What hardly seem materials, down and hair ;
For from men's haunts she nothing seems to win.

Clare.

THE ROBIN.

RT thou the bird whom man loves best,
The pious bird with the scarlet breast,
Our little English Robin ;
The bird that comes about our doors
When autumn winds are sobbing?
Art thou the Peter of Norway boors?
Their Thomas in Finland,
And Russia far inland?
The bird who by some name or other
All men who know thee call thee brother?

Wordsworth.

THE WREN.

THE little woodland dwarf, the tiny Wren,
That from the root-sprigs trills her ditty clear.
Of stature most diminutive herself,
Not so her wondrous house; for, strange to tell!
Hers is the largest structure that is form'd
By tuneful bill and breast. 'Neath some old root,
From which the sloping soil, by wintry rains,
Has been all worn away, she fixes up
Her curious dwelling, close, and vaulted o'er,
And in the side a little gateway porch,
In which (for I have seen) she'll sit and pipe
A merry stave of her shrill roundelay.

Nor always does a single gate suffice
For exit and for entrance to her dome ;
For when (as sometimes haps) within a bush
She builds the artful fabric, then each side
Has its own portico.   But, mark within !
How skilfully the finest plumes and downs
Are softly warp'd ! how closely all around
The outer layers of moss ! each circumstance
Most artfully contrived to favour warmth !
Here read the reason of the vaulted roof ;
Here Providence compensates, ever kind,
The enormous disproportion that subsists
Between the mother and the numerous brood,
Which her small bulk must quicken into life.
Fifteen white spherules, small as moorland hare-bell,
And prettily bespeck'd like fox-glove flower,
Complete her number.   Twice five days she sits,
Fed by her partner, never flitting off,
Save when the morning sun is high, to drink
A dewdrop from the nearest flowret cup.

But now behold the greatest of this train
Of miracles, stupendously minute ;
The numerous progeny, clamant for food,
Supplied by two small bills, and feeble wings
Of narrow range ; supplied, ay, duly fed,
Fed in the dark, and yet not one forgot !

Grahame.

THE ROBIN.

OFT near some single cottage he prefers
To rear his little home ; there, pert and spruce,

He shares the refuse of the goodwife's churn,
Which kindly on the wall for him she leaves :
Below her lintel oft he lights, then in
He boldly flits, and fluttering loads his bill,
And to his young the yellow treasure bears.

Not seldom does he neighbour the low roof
Where tiny elves are taught : a pleasant spot
It is, well fenced from winter blast, and screen'd
By high o'erspreading boughs from summer sun.
Before the door a sloping green extends
No farther than the neighbouring cottage-hedge,
Beneath whose bourtree * shade a little well
Is scoop'd—so limpid, that its guardian trout
(The wonder of the lesser stooping wights)
Is at the bottom seen.

Grahame.

THE SWALLOW.

THE welcome guest of settled spring,
     The Swallow, too, is come at last ;
Just at sunset, when thrushes sing,
I saw her dash with rapid wing,
     And hail'd her as she pass'd.

Come, summer visitant, attach
     To my reed roof your nest of clay,
And let my ear your music catch
Low twittering underneath the thatch,
     At the green dawn of day.

Charlotte Smith.

* Elder Tree.

THE BLACKBIRD.

BLACKBIRD ! sing me something well :
  While all the neighbours shoot thee round,
  I keep smooth plots of fruitful ground,
Where thou may'st warble, eat, and dwell.

The espaliers and the standards all
  Are thine ; the range of lawn and park :
  The unnetted black-hearts ripen dark,
All thine, against the garden wall.

Yet, though I spared thee kith and kin,
  Thy sole delight is sitting still,
  With that gold dagger of the bill
To fret the summer jennetin.

A golden bill ! the silver tongue,
  Cold February loved, is dry ;
  Plenty corrupts the melody
That made thee famous once, when young :

And in the sultry garden squares,
  Now thy flute-notes are changed to coarse,
  I hear thee not at all, or hoarse
As when a hawker hawks his wares.

Take warning ! he that will not sing
  While yon sun prospers in the blue,
  Shall sing for want, ere leaves are new,
Caught in the frozen palms of Spring.

Tennyson.

45

THE GOLDFINCH.

GOLDFINCH, pride of woodland glade,
In thy jet and gold array'd ;
Gentle bird, that lov'st to feed
On the thistle's downy seed ;
Freely frolic, lightly sing,
In the sunbeam spread thy wing !
Spread thy plumage, trim and gay,
Glittering in the noontide ray !
As upon the thorn-tree's stem
Perch'd, thou sipp'st the dewy gem.
Fickle bird, for ever roving,
Endless changes ever loving ;
Now in orchards gaily sporting,
Now to flowery fields resorting ;
Chasing now the thistle's down,
By the gentle zephyrs blown ;
Lightly on thou winn'st thy way,
Always happy, always gay.

From " Time's Telescope."

THE GOLDFINCH.

I LOVE to see the little Goldfinch pluck
The grounsel's feather'd seed, and twit, and twit ;
And then, in bower of apple-blossoms perch'd,
Trim his gay suit, and pay us with a song.
I would not hold him pris'ner for the world.

Hurdis.

46

BIRDS IN MAY.

'T was then those pleasant hours,
When village girls, to hail propitious May,
Search the wild copses and the fields for flowers,
And gaily sing the yellow meads among,
And every heart is cheer'd, and all look fresh and
    young.

His nest amid the orchard's painted buds
   The bullfinch wove ; and loudly sung the thrush
In the green hawthorn ; and the new-leaved woods,
   The golden furze, and holly's guarded bush,
With song resounded : tree-moss grey enchased
   The chaffinch's soft house ; and the dark yew
Received the hedge-sparrow, that careful placed
   Within its bosom eggs as brightly blue
As the calm sky, or the unruffled deep,
   When not a cloud appears, and ev'n the zephyrs sleep.
                       Charlotte Smith.

THE LINNET.

I WADNA gie the Lintie's sang,
   So merry on the broomy lea,
For a' the notes that ever rang
   From a' the harps o' minstrelsy !

Mair dear to me where buss or breer
   Amang the pathless heather grows,
The Lintie's wild, sweet note to hear,
   As on the ev'ning breeze it flows.
                      Anon.

TO DAFFODILS.

FAIR daffodils, we weep to see
　　You haste away so soon ;
As yet, the early-rising sun
　　Has not attain'd its noon.
　　　　Stay, stay,
　　Until the hastening day
　　　　Has run
　　But to the even song ;
And having pray'd together, we
　　Will go with you along.

We have short time to stay as you,
　　We have as short a spring ;
As quick a growth to meet decay,
　　As you or anything.
　　　　We die,
　　As your hours do, and dry
　　　　Away,
　　Like to the summer's rain,
Or as the pearls of morning's dew,
　　Ne'er to be found again.　　　*Herrick.*

ARRANGEMENTS OF A BOUQUET.

ERE damask roses, white and red,
　　Out of my lap first take I ;
Which still shall run along the thread,
　　My chiefest flower this make I.

Among these roses in a row,
　　Next place I pinks in plenty,
These double pansies then for show,
　　And will not this be dainty ?

The pretty pansy then I'll tie,
　　Like stones some chain enchasing ;
And next to them, their near ally,
　　The purple violet placing.

The curious choice clove July flower,
　　Whose kind hight the carnation,
For sweetness of most sovereign power,
　　Shall help my wreath to fashion ;

Whose sundry colours of one kind,
  First from one root derived,
Them in their several suits I'll bind :
  My garland so contrived.

A course of cowslips then I'll stick,
  And here and there (so sparely)
The pleasant primrose down I'll prick,
  Like pearls that will show rarely ;

Then with these marigolds I'll make
  My garland somewhat swelling,
These honeysuckles then I'll take,
  Whose sweets shall help their smelling.

The lily and the fleur-de-lis,
  For colour much contending,
For that I them do only prize.
  They are but poor in scenting ;

The daffodil most dainty is,
  To match with these in meetness ;
The columbine compared to this,
  All much alike for sweetness.

These in their natures only are
  Fit to emboss the border,
Therefore I'll take especial care
  To place them in their order :

Sweet-williams, campions, sops-in-wine,
  One by another neatly :
Thus have I made this wreath of mine,
  And finished it featly.

                                      Drayton.

TO THE BRAMBLE FLOWER.

T HY fruit full well the schoolboy knows,
Wild bramble of the brake!

So, put thou forth thy small white rose ;
  I love it for his sake.
Though woodbines flaunt and roses glow
  O'er all the fragrant bowers,
Thou need'st not be ashamed to show
  Thy satin-threaded flowers ;
For dull the eye, the heart is dull
  That cannot feel how fair,
Amid all beauty, beautiful
  Thy tender blossoms are !
How delicate thy gauzy frill !
  How rich thy branchy stem !
How soft thy voice, when woods are still,
  And thou sing'st hymns to them !
While silent showers are falling slow
  And, 'mid the general hush,
A sweet air lifts the little bough,
  Lone whispering through the bush !
The primrose to the grave is gone ;
  The hawthorn flower is dead ;
The violet by the moss'd grey stone
  Hath laid her weary head ;
But thou, wild bramble ! back dost bring,
  In all their beauteous power,
The fresh green days of life's fair spring,
  And boyhood's blossomy hour.
Scorn'd bramble of the brake ! once more
  Thou bidd'st me be a boy,
To rove with thee the woodlands o'er,
  In freedom and in joy.

Elliott.

FLOWERS.

SENSITIVE plant in a garden grew,
And the young winds fed it with silver dew ;
And it opened its fan-like leaves to the light,
And closed them beneath the kisses of night.

And the spring arose on the garden fair,
Like the spirit of love, felt everywhere !
And each flower and herb on earth's dark
    breast
Rose from the dreams of its wintry rest.

The snowdrop, and then the violet,
Arose from the ground with warm rain wet ;
And their breath was mix'd with fresh odour,
    sent
From the turf, like the voice to the instrument.

Then the pied wind-flowers, and the tulip tall,
And narcissi, the fairest among them all —
Who gaze on their eyes in the stream's recess
Till they die of their own dear loveliness !

And the naiad-like lily of the vale,
Whom youth makes so fair, and passion so pale,
That the light of its tremulous bells is seen
Through their pavilions of tender green ;

And the hyacinth, purple, and white, and blue,
Which flung from its bells a sweet peal anew
Of music so delicate, soft, and intense,
It was felt like an odour within the sense ;

And the rose like a nymph to the bath addrest,
Which unveil'd the depth of her glowing breast,
Till, fold after fold, to the fainting air
The soul of her beauty and love lay bare ;

And the wand-like lily, which lifted up,
As a mœnad, its moonlight-colour'd cup,
Till the fiery star, which is its eye,
Gazed through clear dew on the tender sky ;

And the jessamine faint, and the sweet tuberose,
The sweetest flower for scent that blows !
And rare blossoms from every clime,
Grew in that garden in perfect prime.

And the sinuous paths of lawn and moss
Which led through the garden along and across—
Some open at once to the sun and the breeze,
Some lost among bowers of blossoming trees—

Were all paved with daisies and delicate bells
As fair as the fabulous asphodels,
And flowrets which, drooping as day droop'd too,
Fell into pavilions white, purple, and blue,
To roof the glow-worm from the evening dew.

Shelley.

WILD FLOWERS.

I STOOD tiptoe upon a little hill;
The air was cooling, and so very still,

That the sweet buds with which a modest pride
Fell droopingly in slanting curve aside,
Their scanty-leaved and finely-tapering stems
Had not yet lost their starry diadems,
Caught from the early sobbings of the morn.
The clouds were pure and white as flocks new shorn,
And fresh from the clear brook; sweetly they slept
On the blue fields of heaven and then there crept
A little noiseless noise among the leaves,
Born of the very sigh that silence heaves;
For not the faintest motion could be seen
Of all the shades that slanted o'er the green.
There was wide wandering for the greediest eye,
To peer about upon variety;
Far round the horizon's crystal air to skim,
And trace the dwindled edgings of its brim;
To picture out the quaint and curious bending
Of a fresh woodland valley never-ending:
Or by the bowery clefts and leafy shelves,
Guess where the jaunty streams refresh themselves.
I gazed awhile, and felt as light and free
As though the fanning wings of Mercury
Had play'd upon my heels: I was light-hearted,
And many pleasures to my vision started;
So I straightway began to pluck a posy
Of luxuries bright, milky, soft, and rosy.
A bush of May flowers with the bees about them;
Ah, sure no tasteful nook could be without them;
And let a lush laburnum oversweep them,
And let long grass grow round the roots, to keep them
Moist, cool, and green; and shade the violets,
That they may bind the moss in leafy nets.

   A filbert-edge with wild-brier overtwined,
And clumps of woodbine taking the soft wind
Upon their summer thrones; there too should be

The frequent checker of a youngling tree,
That with a score of bright-green brethren shoots
From the quaint mossiness of aged roots :
Round which is heard a springhead of clear waters,
Prattling so wildly of its lovely daughters,
The spreading blue-bells : it may haply mourn
That such fair clusters should be rudely torn
From their fresh beds, and scatter'd thoughtlessly
By infant hands left on the path to die.
Open afresh your round of starry folds,
Ye ardent marigolds !
Dry up the moisture from your golden lids,
For great Apollo bids
That in these days your praises should be sung
On many harps, which he has lately strung ;
And when again your dewiness he kisses,
Tell him, I have you in my world of blisses :
So haply when I rove in some far vale,
His mighty voice may come upon the gale.

    Here are sweet-peas, on tiptoe for a flight,
With wings of gentle flush o'er delicate white,
And taper fingers catching at all things,
To bind them all about with tiny rings.
What next ? A turf of evening primroses,
O'er which the mind may hover till it dozes ;
O'er which it well might take a pleasant sleep,
But that 'tis ever startled by the leap
Of buds into ripe flowers.

Keats.

THE ROSE.

O, lovely rose!
  Tell her that wastes her time and me,
    That now she knows,
  When I resemble her to thee,
  How sweet and fair she seems to be.

    Tell her that's young,
  And shuns to have her graces spied,
    That hadst thou sprung
In deserts where no men abide,
Thou must have uncommended died.

    Small is the worth
Of beauty from the light retired ;
    Bid her come forth,
Suffer herself to be desired,
And not blush so to be admired.

    Then die, that she
The common fate of all things rare
    May read in thee ;
How small a part of time they share
That are so wondrous sweet and fair !

    Yet, though thou fade,
From thy dead leaves let fragrance rise ;
    And teach the maid
That goodness Time's rude hand defies ;
That virtue lives when beauty dies.

Waller.

THE PRIMROSE.

WELCOME, pale primrose, starting up between
    Dead matted leaves of ash and oak, that strew
    The every lawn, the wood and spinney through,
'Mid creeping moss and ivy's darker green ;
    How much thy presence beautifies the ground !
How sweet thy modest unaffected pride
Glows on the sunny bank, and wood's warm side !
    And when thy fairy flowers in groups are found,
The schoolboy roams enchantingly along,
    Plucking the fairest with a rude delight ;
While the meek shepherd stops his simple song,
    To gaze a moment on the pleasing sight,
O'erjoy'd to see the flowers that truly bring
The welcome news of sweet returning Spring !   *Clare.*

TO THE SWEET-BRIER.

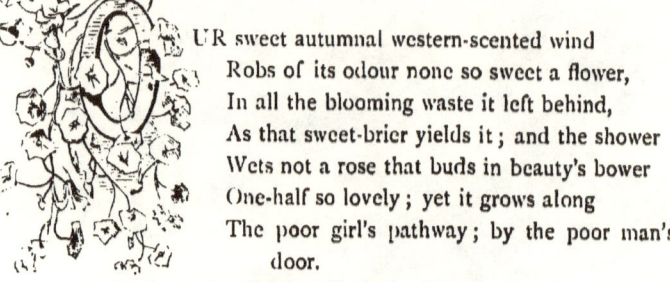

OUR sweet autumnal western-scented wind
   Robs of its odour none so sweet a flower,
In all the blooming waste it left behind,
   As that sweet-brier yields it; and the shower
   Wets not a rose that buds in beauty's bower
One-half so lovely; yet it grows along
   The poor girl's pathway; by the poor man's
      door.
Such are the simple folks it dwells among;
And humble as the bud, so humble be the song.

I love it, for it takes its untouch'd stand
   Not in the vase that sculptors decorate;
Its sweetness all is of my native land;
   And e'en its fragrant leaf has not its mate
   Among the perfumes which the rich and great
Bring from the odours of the spicy East.
   You love your flowers and plants, and will you hate
   The little four-leaved rose that I love best,
That freshest will awake, and sweetest go to rest?

Brainard.

WILD FLOWERS.

I DREAM'D that, as I wander'd by the way,
   Bare winter suddenly was changed to spring,
And gentle odours led my steps astray,
   Mix'd with a sound of waters murmuring
Along a shelving bank of turf, which lay
   Under a copse, and hardly dared to fling
Its green arms round the bosom of the stream,
But kiss'd it and then fled, as thou might'st in a dream.

There grew pied wind-flowers and violets ;
   Daisies, those pearl'd Arcturi of the earth,
The constellated flower that never sits ;
   Faint oxlips ; tender blue-bells, at whose birth
The sod scarce heaved, and that tall flower that wets
Its mother's face with heaven-collected tears,
When the low wind, its playmate's voice, it hears.

And in the warm hedge grew lush eglantine,
   Green cowbind and the moonlight-colour'd May,
And cherry blossoms, and white cups, whose wine
   Was the bright dew yet drain'd not by the day ;
And wild roses, and ivy serpentine,
   With its dark buds and leaves, wandering astray,
And flowers azure, black, and streak'd with gold ;
Fairer than any waken'd eyes behold.

And nearer to the river's trembling edge
   There grew broad flag-flowers, purple prankt with white,
And starry river buds among the sedge,
   And floating water-lilies, broad and bright,
Which lit the oak that overhung the edge
   With moonlight beams of their own watery light ;
And bulrushes and reeds of such deep green
As soothed the dazzled eye with sober sheen.

Methought that of these visionary flowers
   I made a nosegay, bound in such a way
That the same hues which in their natural bowers
   Were mingled or opposed, the like array
Kept these imprison'd children of the hours
   Within my hand—and then, elate and gay,
I hasten'd to the spot whence I had come,
That I might there present it !—oh, to whom ?

                       Shelley.

DAFFODILS.

I WANDER'D lonely as a cloud
That floats on high o'er vales and hills,
When all at once I saw a crowd,
A host of golden daffodils,
Beside the lake, beneath the trees,
Fluttering and dancing in the breeze.

Continuous as the stars that shine
And twinkle on the milky way,
They stretch'd in never-ending line
Along the margin of a bay :
Ten thousand saw I at a glance
Tossing their heads in sprightly dance.

The waves beside them danced, but they
Out-did the sparkling waves in glee :
A poet could not but be gay,
In such a jocund company ;
I gazed—and gazed—but little thought
What wealth the show to me had brought :

For oft, when on my couch I lie,
In vacant or in pensive mood,
They flash upon that inward eye
Which is the bliss of solitude,
And then my heart with pleasure fills,
And dances with the daffodils.

Wordsworth.

SUMMER.

NOW have young April and the blue-eyed May
  Vanish'd awhile, and lo! the glorious June
  (While nature ripens in his burning noon)
Comes like a young inheritor; and gay,
Although his parent months have pass'd away:
  But his green crown shall wither, and the tune
  That usher'd in his birth be silent soon,
And in the strength of youth shall he decay.
What matters this—so long as in the past
  And in the days to come we live, and feel
  The present nothing worth, until it steal
  Away, and, like a disappointment, die?
  For Joy, dim child of Hope and Memory,
Flies ever on before or follows fast.   *Proctor.*

A JUNE DAY.

WHO has not dream'd a world of bliss,
On a bright sunny noon like this,
Couch'd by his native brook's green maze,
With comrade of his boyish days?
While all around them seem'd to be
Just as in joyous infancy.
Who has not loved, at such an hour,
Upon that heath, in birchen bower,
Lull'd in the poet's dreamy mood,
Its wild and sunny solitude?
While o'er the waste of purple ling
You mark'd a sultry glimmering;
Silence herself there seems to sleep,
Wrapp'd in a slumber long and deep,
Where slowly stray those lonely sheep
Through the tall foxglove's crimson bloom,
And gleaming of the scatter'd broom.
Love you not, then, to list and hear
The crackling of the gorse-flowers near,
Pouring an orange-scented tide
Of fragrance o'er the desert wide?
To hear the buzzard whimpering shrill
Hovering above you high and still?
The twittering of the bird that dwells
Amongst the heath's delicious bells?
While round your bed, or fern and blade,
Insects in green and gold array'd,
The sun's gay tribes have lightly stray'd;
And sweeter sound their humming wings
Than the proud minstrel's echoing strings.

Howitt.

64

THE SUMMER MONTHS.

THEY come! the merry summer months of beauty, love, and flowers;
They come! the gladsome months that bring thick leafiness to bowers.

Up, up, my heart ! and walk abroad, fling work and care
    aside ;
Seek silent hills, or rest thyself where peaceful waters glide ;
Or underneath the shadow vast of patriarchal tree,
See through its leaves the cloudless sky in rapt tranquillity.

The grass is soft ; its velvet touch is grateful to the hand,
And, like the kiss of maiden love, the breeze is sweet and
    bland ;
The daisy and the buttercup are nodding courteously ;
It stirs their blood with kindest love to bless and welcome
    thee.
And mark how with thine own thin locks, they now are
    silvery grey—
That blissful breeze is wantoning, and whispering " Be gay ! "

There is no cloud that sails along the ocean of yon sky
But hath its own wing'd mariners to give it melody.
Thou see'st their glittering fans outspread, all gleaming like
    red gold,
And hark ! with shrill pipe musical, their merry course they
    hold.
God bless them all, these little ones, who, far above this
    earth,
Can make a scoff of its mean joys, and vent a nobler birth.

But soft ! mine ear upcaught a sound—from yonder wood
    it came ;
The spirit of the dim green glade did breathe his own glad
    name.
Yes, it is he ! the hermit bird, that, apart from all his kind,
Slow spells his beads monotonous to the soft western wind.
Cuckoo ! cuckoo ! he sings again—his notes are void of art.
But simplest strains do soonest sound the deep founts of
    the heart.

Good Lord! it is a gracious boon for thought-crazed wight
    like me,
To smell again these summer flowers beneath this summer
    tree!
To suck once more in every breath their little souls away,
And feed my fancy with fond dreams of youth's bright
    summer day;
When rushing forth, like untamed colt, the reckless truant
    boy—
Wandered through green woods all day long, a mighty
    heart of joy!

I'm sadder now—I have had cause; but oh! I'm proud to
    think
That each pure joy-fount loved of yore I yet delight to
    drink;
Leaf, blossom, blade, hill, valley, stream, the calm unclouded
    sky,
Still mingle music with my dreams, as in the days gone by.
When summer's loveliness and light fall round me dark
    and cold,
I'll bear indeed life's heaviest curse, a heart that hath wax'd
    old.

                               Motherwell.

SUMMER.

IS Summer, 'tis Summer, the wild birds are
    singing,
The woods and the glens with their sweet
    notes are ringing;
The skies are all glowing with crimson and
    gold,
    And the trees their bright blossoms begin
    to unfold.
The cushat is breathing his murmurs of love,
The stars are adorning the blue skies above,
While the moon in her beauty is shining on high,
And soothing the heart, while she pleases the eye.

'Tis Summer, 'tis Summer,—and Winter no more
Is heard in the winds, or the ocean's wild roar;
But so calm are the waves over all the great deep,
That their murmurs might lull a young infant to sleep.
The streamlets are gliding all lovely and calm—
And the zephyrs come laden with fragrance and balm;
Then, oh! let us bow to the merciful Power,
Who lives in the sunbeam, the tree, and the flower,
Who stills the wild tempest, and bids the vast sea
Unruffled and calm as a placid lake be—
Let us bow to that God, who gave Summer its birth,
And who scatters His treasures all over the earth,

Anon.

SUMMER TINTS.

HOW sweet I've wander'd bosom-deep in grain,
   When Summer's mellowing pencil sweeps the shade
Of ripening tinges o'er the chequer'd plain :
   Light tawny oat-lands with a yellow blade ;
   And bearded corn like armies in parade ;
Beans lightly scorch'd, that still preserve their green ;
   And nodding lands of wheat in bleachy brown ;
   And streaking banks, where many a maid and clown
Contrast a sweetness to the rural scene,—
   Forming the little haycocks up and down ;
While o'er the face of Nature softly swept
   The lingering wind, mixing the brown and green
So sweet that shepherds from their bowers have crept,
   And stood delighted musing o'er the scene.

Clare.

JULY.

OUD is the Summer's busy song ;
The smallest breeze can find a tongue,
While insects of each tiny size
Grow teasing with their melodies,
Till noon burns with its blistering breath
Around, and day dies still as death.
The busy noise of man and brute
Is on a sudden lost and mute ;
Even the brook that leaps along
Seems weary of its bubbling song,
And so soft its waters creep,
Tired silence sinks in sounder sleep ;
The cricket on its bank is dumb,
The very flies forget to hum ;
And, save the wagon rocking round,
The landscape sleeps without a sound.
The breeze is stopp'd, the lazy bough
Hath not a leaf that danceth now ;
The taller grass upon the hill,
And spider's threads, are standing still ;
The feathers dropp'd from moor-hen's wing,
Which to the water's surface cling,
Are steadfast, and as heavy seem
As stones beneath them in the stream ;
Hawkweed and groundsel's fanny downs
Unruffled keep their seedy crowns ;
And in the oven-heated air
Not one light thing is floating there,
Save that to the earnest eye
The restless heat seems twittering by

Noon swoons beneath the heat it made,
And flowers e'en within the shade,
Until the sun slopes in the west
Like weary traveller, glad to rest
On pillow'd clouds of many hues ;
Then Nature's voice its joy renews,
And chequer'd field and grassy plain
Hum with their summer songs again,
A requiem to the day's decline,
Whose setting sunbeams coolly shine,
As welcome to day's feeble powers
As falling dews to thirsty flowers.

Clare.

SUMMER.

FT when thy season, sweetest queen,
Has drest the groves in livery green ;
When in each fair and fertile field
Beauty begins her bower to build ;
While Evening, veil'd in shadows brown,
Puts her matron-mantle on,
And mists in spreading steams convey
More fresh the fumes of new-shorn hay.

* * * * * * *

There through the dusk but dimly seen,
Sweet evening objects intervene :
His wattled cotes the shepherd plants,
Beneath her elm the milkmaid chants.
The woodman, speeding home, awhile
Rests him at a shady stile.
Nor wants there fragrance to dispense

Refreshment o'er my soothèd sense ;
Nor tangled woodbine's balmy bloom,
Nor grass besprent to breathe perfume :
Nor lurking wild thyme's spicy sweet
To bathe in dew my roving feet ;
Nor wants there note of Philomel,
Nor sound of distant-tinkling bell :
Nor lowings faint of herds remote,
Nor mastiff's bark from bosom'd cot ;
Rustle the breezes lightly borne
O'er deep embattled ears of corn ;
Round ancient elm, with humming noise,
Full loud the chaffer-swarms rejoice.
Meantime, a thousand dyes invest
The ruby chambers of the west !
That all aslant the village tower
A mild reflected radiance pour,
While, with the level-streaming rays,
Far seen its arched windows blaze :
And the tall grove's green top is dight
In russet tints, and gleams of light :
So that the gay scene by degrees
Bathes my blithe heart in ecstasies ;
And Fancy to my ravish'd sight
Portrays her kindred visions bright.
At length the parting light subdues
My soften'd soul to calmer views,
And fainter shapes of pensive joy,
As twilight dawns, my mind employ,
Till from the path I fondly stray
In musings lapt, nor heed the way ;
Wandering through the landscape still,
Till Melancholy has her fill ;
And on each moss-wove border damp,
The glow-worm hangs his fairy lamp.   *Warton.*

THE VILLAGE INN.

NEAR yonder thorn that lifts its head on high,
Where once the sign-post caught the passing eye,

L

Low lies that house where nut-brown draughts inspired,
Where grey-beard mirth and smiling toil retired,
Where village statesmen talk'd with looks profound,
And news much older than their ale went round.
Imagination fondly stoops to trace
The parlour splendours of that festive place ;
The whitewash'd wall, the nicely sanded floor,
The varnish'd clock that click'd behind the door ;
The chest contrived a double debt to pay,
A bed by night, a chest of drawers by day ;
The pictures placed for ornament and use,
The twelve good rules, the royal game of goose ;
The hearth, except when winter chill'd the day,
With aspen boughs, and flowers, and fennel gay ;
While broken tea-cups, wisely kept for show,
Ranged o'er the chimney, glisten'd in a row.

Goldsmith.

SUMMER.

STOOD upon the hills, when heaven's wide arch
Was glorious with the sun's returning march,
And woods were brighten'd, and soft gales
Went forth to kiss the sun-clad vales.
The clouds were far beneath me ; bathed in light,
They gather'd mid-day round the wooded height,
And, in their fading glory, shone
Like hosts in battle overthrown,

As many a pinnacle, with shifting glance,
Through the grey mist thrust up its shatter'd lance,
And rocking on the cliff was left
The dark pine, blasted, bare, and cleft.
The veil of cloud was lifted, and below
Glow'd the rich valley, and the river's flow
Was darken'd by the forest's shade,
Or glisten'd in the white cascade ;
Where upward, in the mellow blush of day,
The noisy bittern wheel'd his spiral way.

I heard the distant waters dash,
I saw the current whirl and flash,—
And richly, by the blue lake's silver beach,
The woods were bending with a silent reach.
Then o'er the vale, with gentle swell,
The music of the village bell
Came sweetly to the echo-giving hills ;
And the wild horn, whose voice the woodland fills,
Was ringing to the merry shout
That faint and far the glen sent out,
Where, answering to the sudden shot, thin smoke,
Through thick-leaved branches, from the dingle broke.
If thou art worn and hard beset
With sorrows, that thou wouldst forget,—
If thou wouldst read a lesson, that will keep
Thy heart from fainting and thy soul from sleep,
Go to the woods and hills !—No tears
Dim the sweet look that Nature wears.

Longfellow.

JUNE.

THE summer-time has come again,
  With all its light and mirth,
And June leads on the laughing hours
  To bless the weary earth.

The sunshine lies along the street,
  So dim and cold before,
And in the open window creeps,
  And slumbers on the floor.

The country was so fresh and fine,
  And beautiful in May,
It must be more than beautiful—
  A Paradise to day !

If I were only there again,
  I'd seek the lanes apart,
And shout aloud in mighty words,
  To ease my happy heart.   *Stoddard.*

FLOCKS AND HERDS.

AROUND th' adjoining brook, that purls along
The vocal grove, now fretting o'er a rock,
Now scarcely moving through a reedy pool,
Now starting to a sudden stream, and now
Gently diffused into a limpid plain,
A various group the herds and flocks compose,
Rural confusion! On the grassy bank
Some ruminating lie; while others stand
Half in the flood, and often bending sip
The circling surface. In the middle droops
The strong laborious ox, of honest front,
Which incomposed he shakes; and from his sides
The troublous insects lashes with his tail,
Returning still. Amid his subjects safe,
Slumbers the monarch-swain, his careless arm
Thrown round his head, on downy moss sustain'd :
Here laid his scrip, with wholesome viands fill'd ;
There, listening every noise, his watchful dog.

Thomson.

THE SHEPHERD.

H ! gentle Shepherd ! thine the lot to tend,
Of all that feels distress, the most assail'd,
Feeble, defenceless : lenient be thy care :
But spread around thy tenderest diligence
In flowery spring-time, when the new-dropp'd lamb,
Tottering with weakness by his mother's side,
Feels the fresh world about him ; and each thorn,
Hillock, or furrow, trips his feeble feet :
Oh, guard his meek sweet innocence from all
Th' innumerous ills that rush around his life ;
Mark the quick kite, with beak and talons prone,
Circling the skies to snatch him from the plain ;
Observe the lurking crows ; beware the brake,—
There the sly fox the careless minute waits ;
Nor trust thy neighbour's dog, nor earth, nor sky :
Thy bosom to a thousand cares divide :
Eurus oft flings his hail ; the tardy fields
Pay not their promised food ; and oft the dam
O'er her weak twins with empty udder mourns,
Or fails to guard, when the bold bird of prey
Alights, and hops in many turns around,
And tires her also turning : to her aid
Be nimble, and the weakest in thine arms
Gently convey to the warm cot, and oft,
Between the lark's note and the nightingale's,
His hungry bleating still with tepid milk ;—
In this soft office may thy children join,
And charitable actions learn in sport.
Nor yield him to himself, ere vernal airs
Sprinkle the little croft with daisy flowers :
Nor yet forget him : life has rising ills.   *Dyer.*

THE SHEPHERD'S LIFE.

THRICE, oh, thrice happy shepherd's life and state,
When courts are happiness' unhappy pawns !
His cottage low, and safely humble gate
Shuts out proud Fortune, with her scorns and fawns.
    No fearèd treason breaks his quiet sleep :
    Singing all day, his flocks he learns to keep ;
Himself as innocent as are his simple sheep.

No Serian worms he knows, that with their thread
Draw out their silken lives ; nor silken pride :
His lambs' warm fleece well fits his little need,
Not in that proud Sidonian tincture dyed :
    No empty hopes, no courtly fears him fright,
    Nor begging wants his middle fortune bite ;
But sweet content exiles both misery and spite.

79

Instead of music and base flattering tongues,
Which wait to first salute my lord's uprise ;
The cheerful lark wakes him with early songs,
And birds' sweet whistling notes unlock his eyes :
 In country plays is all the strife he uses,
 Or sing or dance unto the rural Muses ;
And, but in music's sports, all difference refuses.

His certain life, that never can deceive him,
Is full of thousand sweets and rich content :
The smooth-leaved beeches in the field receive him
With coolest shades, till noontide's rage is spent :
 His life is neither tost in boist'rous seas
 Of troublous world, nor lost in slothful ease ;
Pleased and full bless'd he lives, when he his God can please.

His bed of wool yields safe and quiet sleeps,
While by his side his faithful spouse hath place :
His little son into his bosom creeps,
The lively picture of his father's face :
 Never his humble house or state torment him ;
 Less he could like, if less his God had sent him ;
And when he dies, green turfs with grassy tomb content him.
        Phineas Fletcher.

FROM THE "FAITHFUL SHEPHERDESS."

SHEPHERDS all, and maidens fair,
Fold your flocks up, for the air
'Gins to thicken, and the sun
Already his great course hath run.
See the dew-drops, how they kiss
Every little flower that is

Hanging on their velvet heads,
Like a rope of crystal beads ;
See the heavy clouds low falling,
And bright Hesperus down calling
The dead night from underground ;
At whose rising, mists unsound,
Damps and vapours fly apace,
Hovering o'er the wanton face
Of those pastures where they come
Striking dead both bud and bloom.
Therefore, from such danger lock
Every one his lovèd flock ;
And let your dogs lie loose without,
Lest the wolf come as a scout
From the mountain, and, ere day,
Bear a lamb or kid away ;
Or the crafty, thievish fox
Break upon your simple flocks.
To secure yourself from these,
Be not too secure in ease ;
Let one eye his watches keep,
While the other eye doth sleep ;
So you shall good shepherds prove,
And for ever hold the love
Of our great God.   Sweetest slumbers,
And soft silence, fall in numbers
On your eyelids ! so farewell !
Thus I end my evening knell !

John Fletcher.

LAMBS AT PLAY.

Say, ye that know, ye who have felt and seen
Spring's morning smiles, and soul-enlivening green,—
Say, did you give the thrilling transport way?
Did your eye brighten, when young lambs, at play,
Leap'd o'er your path with animated pride,
Or gazed in merry clusters by your side?
Ye who can smile, to wisdom no disgrace,
At the arch meaning of a kitten's face,
If spotless innocence and infant mirth
Excite to praise, or give reflection birth,
In shades like these pursue your favourite joy
'Midst nature's revel, sports that never cloy.—
A few begin a short but vigorous race,
And indolence, abash'd, soon flies the place:
Thus challenged forth, see thither, one by one,
From every side assembling playmates run;

A thousand wily antics mark their stay,
A starting crowd impatient of delay.
Like the fond dove from fearful prison freed,
Each seems to say, " Come, let us try our speed."
Away they scour, impetuous, ardent, strong,
The green turf trembling as they bound along ;
Adown the slope, then up the hillock climb,
Where every molehill is a bed of thyme ;
There panting stop, yet scarcely can refrain, —
A bird, a leaf will set them off again.
Or, if a gale with strength unusual blow,
Scattering the wild-brier roses into snow,
Their little limbs increasing efforts try,
Like the torn flower, the fair assemblage fly.
Ah, fallen rose ! sad emblem of their doom ;
Frail as thyself, they perish while they bloom !

Bloomfield.

FOREST WALKS.

EHOLD yon pool, by unexhausted springs
Still nurtured, draw the multitude that gaze
The plains adjacent ! On the bank worn bare,
And printed with ten thousand steps, the colts
In shifting groups combine, or, to the brink
Descending, dip their pasterns in the wave.
Bolder the horned tribes, far from the shore,
Immerge their chests ; and while the hungry swarm
Now soars aloof, now resolute descends,
Lash their tormented sides, by insects pierced.
. . . . . They stand,
Each in his place, save when some wearied beast

The pressure of the crowd no longer brooks,
Or in mere vagrant mood her station quits
Restless; or some intruder from afar
Flying o'er hill and plain the gadfly's sting,
(For still the dreaded hum she hears, and shakes
The air with iterated lowings,) spies
The watery gleam.   With wildly tossing head,
And tail projecting far, and maddening gait,
She plunges in, and breaks the ranks and spreads
Confusion, till constrain'd at length she stops.

Gisborne.

SONG.

WIFTLY turn the murmuring wheel!
    Night has brought the welcome hour,
When the weary fingers feel
    Help as if from fairy power;
Dewy night o'ershades the ground,—
Turn the swift wheel round and round.

Now beneath the starry sky
    Rest the widely scatter'd sheep;
Ply the pleasant labour, ply;
    For the spindle, while they sleep,
With a motion smooth and fine,
Gathers up a trustier line.

Short-lived likings may be bred
    By a glance of feeble eyes;
But true love is like the thread
    Which the kindly wool supplies,
When the flocks are all at rest,
Sleeping on the mountain's breast.—*Wordsworth.*

SHEARING-TIME.

J F verdant elder spreads
Her silver flowers ; if humble daisies yield

To yellow crowfoot and luxuriant grass,
Gay shearing-time approaches.   First, howe'er,
Drive to the double fold, upon the brim
Of a clear river ; gently drive the flock,
And plunge them one by one into the flood.
Plunged in the flood, not long the struggler sinks,
With his white flakes, that glisten through the tide ;
The sturdy rustic, in the middle wave
Awaits to seize him rising ; one arm bears
His lifted head above the limpid stream,
While the full, clammy fleece the other laves
Around, laborious with repeated toil,
And then resigns him to the sunny bank,
Where, bleating loud, he shakes his dripping locks.

Dyer.

RURAL SCENERY

COUNTRY LIFE.

HAPPY the man who has the town escaped!
To him the whistling trees, the murmuring brooks,
  The shining pebbles, preach
  Virtue's and wisdom's lore.

The whispering grove a holy temple is
To him, where God draws nigher to his soul
  Each verdant sod a shrine,
  Whereby he kneels to Heaven.

The nightingale on him sings slumber down—
The nightingale rewakes him, fluting sweet,
  When shines the lovely red
  Of morning through the trees.

Then he admires thee in the plain, O God !
In the ascending pomp of dawning day—
    Thee in the glorious sun—
    The worm—the budding branch.

Where coolness gushes in the waving grass,
Or o'er the flowers, streams, and fountains rests ;
    Inhales the breath of prime,
    The gentle airs of eve.

His straw deck'd thatch, where doves bask in the sun,
And play and hop, incites to sweeter rest
    Than golden halls of state
    Or beds of down afford.

To him the plumy-people sporting chirp,
Chatter, and whistle, on his basket perch,
    And from his quiet hand
    Pick crumbs, or peas, or grains.

Oft wanders he alone, and thinks on death ;
And in the village churchyard by the graves
    Sits, and beholds the cross—
    Death's waving garland there.

The stone beneath the elders, where a text
Of Scripture teaches joyfully to die—
    And with his scythe stands Death—
    An angel, too, with palms.

Happy the man who thus hath 'scaped the town !
Him did an angel bless when he was born—
    The cradle of the boy
    With flowers celestial strew'd.

Hölty.

THE HAMLET.

THE hinds how blest, who ne'er beguiled
To quit their hamlet's hawthorn wild,

Nor haunt the crowd, nor tempt the main,
For splendid care and guilty gain !

When morning's twilight-tinctured beam
Strikes their low thatch with slanting gleam,
They rove abroad in ether blue,
To dip the scythe in fragrant dew ;
The sheaf to bind, the beech to fell,
That nodding shades a craggy dell.

'Midst gloomy glades, in warbles clear,
Wild Nature's sweetest notes they hear :
On green untrodden banks they view
The hyacinth's neglected hue ;
In their lone haunts, and woodland rounds,
They spy the squirrel's airy bounds ;
And startle from her ashen spray,
Across the glen, the screaming jay :
Each native charm their steps explore
Of solitude's sequester'd store.

For them the moon with cloudless ray
Mounts, to illume their homeward way :
Their weary spirits to relieve,
The meadows incense breathe at eve.
No riot mars the simple fare,
That o'er a glimmering hearth they share :
But when the curfew's measured roar
Duly, the darkening valleys o'er,
Has echoed from the distant town,
They wish no beds of cygnet-down,
No trophied canopies, to close
Their drooping eyes in quick repose.

Their little sons, who spread the bloom
Of health around the clay-built room,

Or through the primrosed coppice stray,
Or gambol in the new-mown hay ;
Or quaintly braid the cowslip-twine,
Or drive afield the tardy kine ;
Or hasten from the sultry hill,
To loiter at the shady rill ;
Or climb the tall pine's gloomy crest,
To rob the raven's ancient nest.

Their humble porch with honey'd flowers
The curling woodbine's shade embowers ;
From the small garden's thymy mound
Their bees in busy swarms resound ;
Nor fell Disease, before his time,
Hastes to consume life's golden prime.
But when their temples long have wore
The silver crown of tresses hoar,
As studious still calm peace to keep,
Beneath a flowery turf they sleep.

Warton.

A RURAL SCENE.

HROUGH a beech wood the path—
A wild rude copse road—winds beneath the
    light
And feathery stems of the young trees, so
    fresh
In their new delicate green, and so contrast-
    ing,
With their slim flexile forms, that almost seem
To bend as the wind passes, with the firm

Deep-rooted vigour of those older trees
And nobler,—those grey giants of the woods,
That stir not at the tempest. Oh, that path
Is pleasant, with its beds of richest moss,
And tufts of fairest flowers ; fragrant woodroof
So silver white ; wood-sorrel elegant,
Or light anemone. A pleasant path
Is that, and such a sense of freshness round us,
Of cool and lovely light, the very air
Has the hue of the young leaves ; downward the road
Winds still beneath a beech, whose slender stem
Seems toss'd across the path ; all suddenly
The close wood ceases, and a steep descent
Leads to a valley, whose opposing side
Is crown'd with answering woods ; a narrow valley
Of richest meadow land, which creeps half up
The opposite hill, and in the midst a farm
With its old ample orchard, now one flush
Of fragrant bloom, and just beneath the wood,
Close by the house a rude deserted chalk-pit,
Half full of rank and creeping plants, with briars
And pendent roots of trees half covered o'er,
Like some wild shaggy ruin. Beautiful
To me is that low farm. There is a peace,
A deep repose, a silent harmony,
Of nature and of man. The circling woods
Shut out all human eyes ; and the gay orchard
Spreads its sweet world of blossoms, all unseen,
Save by the smiling sky. That were a spot
To live and die in.

Mitford.

RURAL PLEASURES.

HERE happy would they stray in summer hours,
To spy the birds in their green leafy bowers,

And learn their various voices; to delight
In the gay tints and ever-bickering flight
Of dragon-flies upon the river's brim ;
Or swift kingfisher in his gaudy trim
Come skimming past, with a shrill, sudden cry ;
Or on the river's sunny marge to lie,
And count the insects that meandering trace,
In some smooth nook, their circuits on its face.
Now gravely ponder on the frothy cells
Of insects, hung on flowery pinnacles ;
Now, wading the deep grass, exulting trace
The corncrake's curious voice from place to place ;
Now here—now there—now distant—now at hand—
Now hush'd, just where in wondering mirth they stand.
To lie abroad on Nature's lonely breast,
Amidst the music of a summer's sky,
Where tall, dark pines the northern bank invest
Of a still lake ; and see the long pikes lie
Basking upon the shallows ; with dark crest,
And threatening pomp, the swan go sailing by ;
And many a wild fowl on its breast that shone,
Flickering, like liquid silver, in the joyous sun ;
The duck, deep poring with her downward head,
Like a buoy floating on the ocean wave ;
The Spanish goose, like drops of crystal, shed
The water o'er him, his rich plumes to lave ;
The beautiful widgeon, springing upward, spread
His clapping wings ; the heron stalking grave
Into the stream ; the coot and water-hen
Vanish into the flood, then, far off, rise again :—
Such were their joys !

Howitt.

A WISH.

MINE be a cot beside the hill ;
A bee-hive's hum shall soothe my ear
A willowy brook that turns a mill,
With many a fall shall linger near.

The swallow oft, beneath my thatch,
Shall twitter from her clay-built nest ;
Oft shall the pilgrim lift the latch,
And share my meal, a welcome guest.

Around my ivied porch shall spring
Each fragrant flower that drinks the dew ;
And Lucy at her wheel shall sing,
In russet gown and apron blue.

The village church among the trees,
Where first our marriage vows were given,
With merry peals shall swell the breeze,
And point with taper spire to heaven.

Rogers.

AN ENGLISH SCENE.

HOW oft upon yon eminence our pace
Has slacken'd to a pause, and we have borne
The ruffling wind, scarce conscious that it blew ;
While Admiration, feeding at the eye,
And still unsated, dwelt upon the scene !
Thence with what pleasure have we just discern'd

95

The distant plough slow moving, and beside
His labouring team, that swerved not from the track,
The sturdy swain diminish'd to a boy !
Here Ouse, slow winding through a level plain
Of spacious meads with cattle sprinkled o'er,
Conducts the eye along his sinuous course,
Delighted.   There, fast rooted in their bank,
Stand, never overlook'd, our favourite elms,
That screen the herdsman's solitary hut ;
While far beyond, and overthwart the stream,
That, as with molten glass, inlays the vale,
The sloping land recedes into the clouds,
Displaying on its varied side the grace
Of hedge-row beauties numberless,—square tower,
Tall spire, from which the sound of cheerful bells
Just undulates upon the listening ear,
Groves, heaths, and smoking villages remote.
Scenes must be beautiful, which daily view'd
Please daily, and whose novelty survives
Long knowledge and the scrutiny of years :
Praise justly due to those that I describe.

Cowper.

A SKETCH.

THE rush-thatch'd cottage on the purple moor,
Where ruddy children frolic round the door ;
The moss-grown antlers of the aged oak,
The shaggy locks that fringe the colt unbroke :
The bearded goat, with nimble eyes that glare
Through the long tissue of his hoary hair,

As with quick foot he climbs some ruin'd wall,
And crops the ivy which prevents its fall ;
With rural charms the tranquil mind delight,
And form a picture to th' admiring sight.

Darwin.

THE EVENING WALK.

———— But see, the setting sun
Puts on a milder countenance, and skirts
The undulated clouds, that cross his way
With glory visible.   His axle cools,
And his broad disk, though fervent, not intense,
Foretells the near approach of matron Night.
Ye fair, retreat !   Your drooping flowers need
Wholesome refreshment.   Down the hedge-row path
We hasten home, and only slack our speed
To gaze a moment at th' accustom'd gap,
That all so unexpectedly presents
The clear cerulean prospect down the vale.
Dispersed along the bottom flocks and herds,
Hay-ricks and cottages, beside a stream,
That silverly meanders here and there ;
And higher up cornfields, and pastures, hops,
And waving woods, and tufts, and lonely oaks,
Thick interspersed as Nature best was pleased.

Happy the man, who truly loves his home,
And never wanders farther from his door

Than we have gone to-day ; who feels his heart

Still drawing homeward, and delights, like us,
Once more to rest his foot on his own threshold.—*Hurdis.*

DEVONSHIRE.

HERE Dart romantic winds its mazy course,
And mossy rocks adhere to woody hills,
From whence each creeping rill its store
    distils,
And wandering waters join with rapid force ;
There Nature's hand has wildly strown her flowers,
And varying prospects strike the roving eyes ;
Rough-hanging woods o'er cultured hills arise ;
   Thick ivy spreads around huge antique towers ;
     And fruitful groves
   Scatter their blossoms fast as falling showers,
   Perfuming every stream which o'er the landscape pours.

Along the grassy banks how sweet to stray,
   When the mild eve smiles in the glowing west,
And lengthen'd shades proclaim departing day,
And fainting sunbeams in the waters play,
   When every bird seeks its accustom'd rest !
How grand to see the burning orb descend,
   And the grave sky wrapp'd in its nightly robes,
   Whether resplendent with the starry globes,
   Or silver'd by the mildly solemn moon ;
   When nightingales their lonely songs resume,
And folly's sons their babbling noise suspend

Or when the darkening clouds fly o'er the sea,
  And early morning beams a cheerful ray,
Waking melodious songsters from each tree ;
    How sweet beneath each dewy hill
    Amid the pleasing shades to stray,
      Where nectar'd flowers their sweets distil,
Whose watery pearls reflect the day !
  To scent the jonquil's rich perfume,
To pluck the hawthorn's tender briers,
    As wild beneath each flowery hedge
    Fair strawberries with violets bloom,
And every joy of spring conspires !

Nature's wild songsters from each bush and tree
  Invite the early walk, and breathe delight :
What bosom heaves not with warm sympathy,
  When the gay lark salutes the new-born light ?
Hark ! where the shrill-toned thrush,
  Sweet whistling, carols the wild harmony !
The linnet warbles, and from yonder bush
  The robin pours soft streams of melody !

Cristall.

NATURE.

LOVE to set me on some steep
  That overhangs the billowy deep,
    And hear the waters roar ;
I love to see the big waves fly,
And swell their bosoms to the sky,
  Then burst upon the shore.

I love, when seated on its brow,
To look o'er all the world below,
  And eye the distant vale ;
From thence to see the waving corn
With yellow hue the hills adorn,
  And bend before the gale.

I love far downward to behold
The shepherd with his bleating fold,
  And hear the tinkling sound
Of little bell and mellow flute,
Wafted on zephyrs soft, now mute,
  Then swell in echoes round.

I love to see, at close of day,
Spread o'er the hills the sun's broad ray,
  While rolling down the west ;
When every cloud in rich attire,
And half the sky, that seems on fire,
  In purple robes is dress'd.

I love, when evening veils the day,
And Luna shines with silver ray,
  To cast a glance around,
And see ten thousand worlds of light
Shine, ever new, and ever bright,
  O'er the vast vault profound.

I love from thence to take my flight,
Far downward on the beams of light,
  And reach my native plain,
Just as the flaming orb of day
Drives night and mists and shades away,
  And cheers the world again.

                              Anon.

AUTUMN.

I SAW old Autumn in the misty morn
Stand shadowless like Silence, listening
To Silence, for no lonely bird would sing
Into his hollow ear from woods forlorn,
Nor lowly hedge, nor solitary thorn ;
Shaking his languid locks, all dewy bright,
With tangled gossamer that fell by night,
   Pearling his coronet of golden corn.

Where are the songs of Summer? With the sun,
Oping the dusky eyelids of the South,
Till shade and silence waken up as one,
And Morning sings with a warm, odorous mouth.

Where are the merry birds?—away, away,
On panting wings, through the inclement skies,
    Lest owls should prey,
    Undazzled at noonday
And tear with horny beak their lustrous eyes

Where are the blooms of Summer? In the West,
Blushing their last to the last sunny hours,
When the mild Eve by sudden Night is prest,
Like tearful Proserpine, snatch'd from her flow'rs
    To a most gloomy breast.
Where is the pride of Summer—the green prime—
The merry, merry leaves all twinkling? There
On the moss'd elm; there on the naked lime
Trembling—and one upon the old oak-tree!
    Where is the Dryad's immortality?
Gone into mournful cypress and dark yew,
Or wearing the long, gloomy Winter through,
    In the smooth holly's green eternity.

The squirrel gloats on his accomplish'd hoard;
The ants have cramm'd their garners with ripe grain,
    And honey-bees have stored
The sweets of Summer in their luscious cells;
The swallows all have wing'd across the main;
But here the Autumn melancholy dwells,
    And sighs her tearful spells
Among the sunless shadows of the plain:
    Alone, alone,
    Upon a mossy stone,
She sits and reckons up the dead and gone
With the last leaves for a lone rosary,
While all the wither'd world looks drearily,
Like a dim picture of the drowned past
In the hush'd mind's mysterious far away,

Doubtful what ghostly thing will steal the last
Into the distance, grey upon the grey.

Oh, go and sit with her, and be o'ershaded
Under the languid downfal of her hair;
She wears a coronal of flowers faded
Upon her forehead, and a face of care.
There is enough of wither'd everywhere
To make her bower, and enough of gloom ;
There is enough of sadness to invite,
If only for the rose that died, whose doom
Is Beauty's—she that with the living bloom
Of conscious cheeks most beautifies the light.
There is enough of sorrowing, and quite
Enough of bitter fruits the earth doth bear—
Enough of chilly droppings from her brow—
Enough of fear and shadowy despair
To frame her cloudy prison for the soul !

Hood

AUTUMN SCENE IN ENGLAND.

BUT see the fading, many-colour'd woods !
Shade deepening over shade the country round
Embrown ; a crowded umbrage, dusk and dun,
Of every hue, from wan declining green
To sooty dark,—these now the lonesome Muse,
Low whispering, lead into their leaf-strown walks,
And give the season in its latest view.

Meantime, light-shadowing all, a sober calm
Fleeces unbounded ether, whose least wave

Stands tremulous, uncertain where to turn
The gentle current; while illumined wide,
The dewy-skirted clouds imbibe the sun,
And through their lucid veil his soften'd force
Shed o'er the peaceful world. Then is the time
For those whom wisdom and whom Nature charm,
To steal themselves from the degenerate crowd,

And soar above this little scene of things;
To tread low-thoughted vice beneath their feet,
To soothe the throbbing passions into peace,
And woo lone Quiet in her silent walks.
 *   *   *   *   *   *
The pale descending year, yet pleasing still,
A gentler mood inspires; for now the leaf

Incessant rustles from the mournful grove ;
Oft startling such as studious walk below,
And slowly circles through the waving air.
But should a quicker breeze amid the boughs
Sob, o'er the sky the leafy deluge streams ;
Till choked and matted with the dreary shower,
The forest-walks, at every rising gale,
Roll wide the wither'd waste, and whistle bleak.
Fled is the blasted verdure of the fields,
And, shrunk into their beds, the flowery race
Their sunny robes resign.   Even what remain'd
Of stronger fruits, falls from the naked tree,
And woods, fields, gardens, orchards, all around
The desolated prospect thrills the soul.

Thomson.

OCTOBER.

Y, thou art welcome, Heaven's delicious breath,
    When woods begin to wear the crimson leaf,
    And suns grow meek, and the meek suns
        grow brief,
    And the year smiles as it draws near its death.
    Wind of the sunny south ! oh still delay
        In the gay woods and in the golden air
        Like to a good old age released from care,
Journeying, in long serenity, away.
In such a bright, late quiet, would that I
    Might wear out life like thee, 'mid bowers and brooks,
    And, dearer yet, the sunshine of kind looks,
And music of kind voices ever nigh ;
And when my last sand twinkled in the glass,
Pass silently from men, as thou dost pass.   *Bryant.*

106

AUTUMN.

ITH what a glory comes and goes the year;
The buds of spring, those beautiful harbingers
Of sunny skies and cloudless times, enjoy
Life's newness and earth's garniture spread
    out;
And when the silver habit of the clouds
Comes down upon the autumn sun, and with
A sober gladness the old year takes up
His bright inheritance of golden fruits,
A pomp and pageant fill the splendid scene.

There is a beautiful spirit breathing now
Its mellow richness on the cluster'd trees,
And, from a beaker full of richest dyes,
Pouring new glory on the autumn woods,
And dipping in warm light the pillar'd clouds.
Morn on the mountain, like a summer bird,
Lifts up her purple wing; and in the vales
The gentle Wind, a sweet and passionate wooer,
Kisses the blushing leaf, and stirs up life
Within the solemn woods of ash deep-crimson'd,
And silver beech, and maple yellow-leaved,
Where Autumn, like a faint old man, sits down
By the wayside a-weary. Through the trees
The golden robin moves. The purple finch,
That on wild cherry and red cedar feeds,
A winter bird, comes with its plaintive whistle,
And pecks by the witch-hazel; whilst aloud

From cottage roofs the warbling blue-bird sings ;
And merrily, with oft-repeated stroke,
Sounds from the thrashing-floor the busy flail.

Oh, what a glory doth this world put on
For him who, with a fervent heart, goes forth
Under the bright and glorious sky, and looks
On duties well peiform'd, and days well spent !
For him the wind, ay, and the yellow leaves,
Shall have a voice, and give him eloquent teachings ;
He shall so hear the solemn hymn, that Death
Has lifted up for all, that he shall go
To his long resting-place without a tear.

Longfellow.

AUTUMN.

SEASON of mists and mellow fruitfulness !
  Close bosom-friend of the maturing sun ;
Conspiring with him how to load and bless
  With fruit the vines that round the thatch-eaves run ;
To bend with apples the moss'd cottage trees,
  And fill all fruit with ripeness to the core ;
    To swell the gourd and plump the hazel-shells
  With a sweet kernel ; to set budding more,
And still more, later flowers for the bees,
Until they think warm days will never cease,
    For summer has o'er-brimmed their clammy cells.

Who hath not seen thee oft amid thy store ?
  Sometimes, whoever seeks abroad may find
Thee sitting careless on a granary floor,
  Thy hair soft-lifted by the winnowing wind ;

Or on a half-reap'd furrow sound asleep,
Drowsed with the fume of poppies, while thy hook

109

Spares the next swath and all its twinèd flowers ;
And sometimes like a gleaner thou dost keep
Steady thy laden head across a brook ;
Or by a cider-press, with patient look,
    Thou watchest the last oozings, hours by hours.

Where are the songs of Spring? Ay, where are they?
    Think not of them, thou hast thy music too,
While barred clouds bloom the soft dying day,
    And touch the stubble-plains with rosy hue ;
Then in a wailful choir the small gnats mourn
    Among the river sallows, borne aloft
        Or sinking as the light wind lives or dies ;
And full-grown lambs loud beat from hilly bourn ;
    Hedge-crickets sing ; and now with treble soft
The redbreast whistles from a garden croft,
    And gathering swallows twitter in the skies.

Keats.

AUTUMN WOODS.

RE in the northern gale,
    The summer tresses of the tree are gone,
    The woods of Autumn all around our vale
        Have put their glory on.

The mountains that infold
    In their wide sweep the colour'd landscape round,
Seem groups of giant kings, in purple and gold,
    That guard the enchanted ground.

AUTUMN.

I roam the woods that crown
The upland, where the mingled splendours glow—
Where the gay company of trees look down
    On the green fields below.

My steps are not alone
In these bright walks ; the sweet south-west, at play,
Flies, rustling, where the painted leaves are strewn
    Along the winding way.

And far in heaven, the while,
The sun that sends that gale to wander here,
Pours out on the fair earth his quiet smile,
    The sweetest of the year.

Where now the solemn shade,
Verdure and gloom, where many branches meet ;
So grateful when the noon of summer made
    The valleys rich with heat?

Let in through all the trees
Come the strange rays ; the forest depths are bright,
Their sunny-colour'd foliage in the breeze
    Twinkles, like beams of light.

The rivulet, late unseen,
Where, bickering through the shrubs, its waters run,
Shines with the image of its golden screen,
    And glimmerings of the sun.

Beneath yon crimson tree,
Lover to listening maid might breathe his flame,
Nor mark within its roseate canopy
    Her blush of maiden shame.

Oh, Autumn, why so soon
Depart the hues that make thy forests glad,
Thy gentle wind, and thy fair sunny noon,
    And leave thee wild and sad !

Ah ! 't were a lot too bless'd
For ever in thy colour'd shades to stray ;
Amid the tresses of the soft south-west,
    To rove and dream for aye ;

And leave the vain, low strife
That makes men mad—the tug for wealth and power,
The passions and the cares that wither life,
    And waste its little hour.

                    Bryant.

OCTOBER.

THE year is now declining; and the air,
When morning blushes on the orient hills,
Embued with icy chillness.   Ocean's wave
Has lost its tepid glow, and slumbering fogs
On clouded days brood o'er its level plain ;
Yet, when the day is at meridian height,
The sun athwart the fading landscape smiles
With most paternal kindness, softly sweet,
And delicately beautiful—a prince
Blessing the realms whose glory comes from him.
   The foliage of the forest, brown and sere,
Drops on the margin of the stubble field,
In which the partridge lingers insecure,
And raises oft, at sombre eventide,

With plaintive throat, her dull and tremulous cry !
The sickle of the husbandman hath ceased,
And left the lap of Nature shorn and bare ;
The odorous clover flowers have disappear'd ;

The yellow pendulous grain is seen no more ;
The perfume of the bean-field has decay'd ;
And roams the wandering bee o'er many a path,
For blossoms which have perish'd. Grassy blades,
Transparent, taper, and of sickly growth,
Shoot, soon to wither, in the sterile fields.

The garden fruits have mellow'd with the year,
And, save the lingering apricot, remains
Nor trace nor token of the summer's wealth !
Yet, on the wild-brier stands the yellow hip ;
And, from the branches of the mountain-ash,
The clustering berries drop their crimson beads
Descending.   On the dark laburnum's sides,
Mix pods of lighter green among the leaves,
Taper, and springless, hasting to decay ;
And on the wintry honeysuckle's stalk
The succulent berries hang.   The robin sits
Upon the mossy gateway, singing clear
A requiem to the glory of the woods.
And, when the breeze awakes, a frequent shower
Of wither'd leaves bestrews the weedy paths,
Or from the branches of the willow whirl,
With rustling sound, upon the turbid stream.

Anon.

AN AUTUMN LANDSCAPE.

AR and wide
        Nature is smiling in her loveliness.
        Masses of wood, green strips of fields, ravines,
        Shown by their outlines drawn against the hills,
        Chimneys and roofs, trees, single and in groups,
        Bright curves of brooks, and vanishing mountain-top,
        Expand upon my sight.   October's brush
        The scene has colour'd ; not with those broad hues
        Mix'd in his later pallet by the frost,
        And dash'd upon the picture till the eye
        Aches with varied splendour, but in tints
Left by light, scatter'd touches.   Overhead
There is a blending of cloud, haze, and sky,

A silvery sheet with spaces of soft blue ;
A trembling veil of gauze is stretch'd athwart
The shadowy hill-sides and dark forest-flanks ;
A soothing quiet broods upon the air,
And the faint sunshine winks with drowsiness.
Far sounds melt mellow on the ear : the bark—
The bleat—the tinkle—whistle—blast of horn—
The rattle of the waggon-wheel—the low—
The fowler's shot—the twitter of the bird,
And e'en the hum of converse from the road.
The grass, with its low insect-tones, appears
As murmuring in its sleep.   This butterfly
Seems as if loth to stir, so lazily
It flutters by.   In fitful starts, and stops,
The locust sings.   The grasshopper breaks out
In brief, harsh strains, amid its pausing chirps.
The beetle, glistening in its sable mail,
Slow climbs the clover-tops, and e'en the ant
Darts round less eagerly.

Street.

SEPTEMBER.

HE meridian sun,
Most sweetly smiling with attemper'd beams,
Sheds gently down a mild and grateful
warmth ;
Beneath its yellow lustre groves and
woods,
Checker'd by one night's frost with various
hues,

While yet no wind has swept a leaf away,
Shine doubly rich.   It were a sad delight
Down the smooth stream to glide, and see it tinged
Upon its brink with all the gorgeous hues,
The yellow, red, or purple of the trees
That, singly, or in tufts, or forests thick,
Adorn the shores ; to see, perhaps, the side
Of some high mount reflected far below,
With its bright colours, intermix'd with spots
Of darker green.   Yes, it were sweetly sad
To wander in the open fields, and hear,
E'en at this hour, the noonday hardly past,
The lulling insects of the summer's night ;
To hear, where lately buzzing swarms were heard,
A lonely bee, long roving here and there
To find a single flower, but all in vain ;
Then rising quick, and with a louder hum,
In widening circles round and round his head,
Straight by the listener flying clear away,
As if to bid the fields a last adieu ;
To hear, within the woodland's sunny side,
Late full of music, nothing, save perhaps
The sound of nutshells, by the squirrel dropp'd
From some tall beech, fast falling through the leaves.

Wilcox.

HARVEST HOME.

SUMMER'S toiling now is past ;
Harvest now hath sent her last—
   Her last, last load.
If the field containeth more,
Master, give it to the poor,
   Abroad—abroad.
Let them through the corn-field roam,
While we welcome harvest-home—
   Harvest-home, harvest-home,—
While we welcome harvest-home :
Songs shall sound and ale-cups foam
   While we welcome harvest-home.   *Miller.*

THE REAPERS.

OON as the morning trembles o'er the sky,
And, unperceived, unfolds the spreading day ;
Before the ripen'd field the reapers stand
In fair array ; each by the lass he loves,
To bear the rougher part, and mitigate
By nameless gentle offices her toil.
At once they stoop and swell the lusty sheaves ;
While through their cheerful band the rural talk,
The rural scandal, and the rural jest,
Fly harmless, to deceive the tedious time,
And steal unfelt the sultry hours away.
Behind the master walks, builds up the shock ;
And, conscious, glancing oft on every side
His sated eye, feels his heart heave with joy.
The gleaners spread around, and here and there,
Spike after spike, their scanty harvest pick.
Be not too narrow, husbandmen ! but fling
From the full sheaf, with charitable stealth,
The liberal handful.   Think, oh, grateful think,
How good the God of Harvest is to you,
Who pours abundance o'er your flowing fields ;
While these unhappy partners of your kind
Wide hover round you, like the fowls of heaven,
And ask their humble dole.

Thomson.

RUTH.

HE stood breast high amid the corn,
Clasp'd by the golden light of morn,
Like the sweetheart of the sun,
Who many a glowing kiss had won.

On her cheek an autumn flush
Deeply ripen'd : such a blush
In the midst of brown was born,
Like red poppies grown with corn.

Round her eyes her tresses fell,
Which were blackest none could tell ;
But long lashes veil'd a light
That had else been all too bright.

And her hat, with shady brim,
Made her tressy forehead dim :
Thus she stood amid the stooks,
Praising God with sweetest looks.

Sure, I said, Heav'n did not mean,
Where I reap thou shouldst but glean ;
Lay thy sheaf adown and come—
Share my harvest and my home.

Hood.

HOCK-CART, OR HARVEST HOME.

COME, sons of summer, by whose toil
We are the lords of wine and oil ;
By whose tough labours, and tough hands,
We rip up first, then reap our lands !
Crown'd with the ears of corn, now come,
And to the pipe sing " Harvest-home."
Come forth, my lord, and see the cart
Drest up with all the country art.
See, here a manikin, there's a sheet
As spotless pure as it is sweet ;
The horses, mares, and frisking fillies,
Clad all in linen white as lilies.
The harvest swains and wenches bound
For joy, to see the hock-cart crown'd.
About the cart hear how the rout
Of rural younglings raise the shout,
Pressing before, some coming after,—
Those with a shout, and these with laughter.
Some bless the cart, some kiss the sheaves,
Some prank them up with oaken leaves ;
Some cross the thill-horse, some with great
Devotion stroke the home-borne wheat !
While other rustics, less attent
To prayers than to merriment,
Run after, with their garments rent.
Well on, brave boys ! to your lord's hearth
Glittering with fire ; where, for your mirth,
Ye shall see first the large and chief
Foundation of your feast—fat beef,

With upper stories—mutton, veal,
And bacon—which makes full the meal ;

With several dishes standing by,—
As here a custard, there a pie,

And here all-tempting frumenty.
And for to make the merry cheer,
If smirking wine be wanting here,
There's that which drowns all care—stout beer ;
Which freely drink to your lord's health,
Then to the plough, the commonwealth ;
Next to your flails, your fanes, your fats ;
Then to the maids with wheaten hats.
To the rough sickle, and crook'd scythe,
Drink, frolic boys, till all be blithe.
Feed and grow fat ; and as ye eat,
Be mindful that the labouring neat.
As you, may have their full of meat ;
And know besides, ye must revoke
The patient ox unto the yoke,
And all go back unto the plough
And harrow, though they're hang'd up now.
And you must know your lord's words true —
Feed him you must whose food fills you ;
And that this pleasure is like rain,
Not sent ye for to drown your pain,
But for to make it spring again.

Herrick.

GLEANING.

ERE, 'midst the boldest triumphs of her worth
Nature herself invites the reapers forth ;
Dares the keen sickle from its twelvemonth's
 rest,
And gives that ardour which in every breast
From infancy to age alike appears,
When the first sheaf its plumy top uprears.

No rake takes here what Heaven to all bestows
Children of want, for you the bounty flows !
And every cottage from the plenteous store
Receives a burden nightly at its door.

 Hark ! where the sweeping scythe now rips along :
Each sturdy mower emulous and strong ;
Whose writhing form meridian heat defies,
Bends o'er his work, and every sinew tries ;
Prostrates the waving treasure at his feet,
But spares the rising clover, short and sweet.
Come, Health ! come, Jollity ! light-footed, come ;
Here hold your revels, and make this your home.
Each heart awaits and hails you as its own ;
Each moisten'd brow, that scorns to wear a frown :
Th' unpeopled dwelling mourns its tenants stray'd ;
E'en the domestic laughing dairy-maid
Hies to the field, the general toil to share.
Meanwhile the Farmer quits his elbow-chair,
His cool brick floor, his pitcher, and his ease,
And braves the sultry beams, and gladly sees
His gates thrown open, and his team abroad,
The ready group attendant on his word,
To turn the swarth, the quiv'ring load to rear,
Or ply the busy rake, the land to clear.
Summer's light garb itself now cumbrous grown,
Each his thin doublet in the shade throws down :
Where oft the mastiff skulks with half-shut eye,
And rouses at the stranger passing by ;
Whilst unrestrain'd the social converse flows,
And every breast Love's powerful impulse knows,
And rival wits with more than rustic grace
Confess the presence of a pretty face.

 For, lo ! encircled there, the lovely Maid,
In youth's own bloom and native smiles array'd ;
Her hat awry, divested of her gown,

Her creaking stays of leather, stout and brown ;
Invidious barrier ! why art thou so high,
When the slight covering of her neck slips by,
There half revealing to the eager sight
Her full, ripe bosom, exquisitely white ?
In many a local tale of harmless mirth,
And many a jest of momentary birth,
She bears a part, and, as she stops to speak,
Strokes back the ringlets from her glowing cheek.
   Now noon gone by, and four declining hours,
The weary limbs relax their boasted pow'rs ;
Thirst rages strong, the fainting spirits fail,
And ask the sov'reign cordial, home-brew'd ale :
Beneath some shelt'ring heap of yellow corn
Rests the hoop'd keg, and friendly cooling horn,
That mocks alike the goblet's brittle frame,
Its costlier potions, and its nobler name.
To *Mary* first the brimming draught is given,
By toil made welcome as the dews of heaven,
And never lip that press'd its homely edge
Had kinder blessings or a heartier pledge.

Bloomfield.

SHOOTING.

.

HERE the rude clamour of the sportsman's joy—
The gun fast thundering, and the winded horn—
Would tempt the muse to sing the rural game ;
How in his mid-career the spaniel, struck
Stiff by the tainted gale, with open nose
Outstretch'd, and finely sensible, draws full,
Fearful, and cautious, on the latent prey :

As in the sun the circling covey bask
Their varied plumes, and, watchful every way,
Through the rough stubble turn the secret eye,

125

Caught in the meshy snare, in vain they beat
Their idle wings, entangled more and more ;
Nor on the surges of the boundless air,
Though borne triumphant, are they safe ; the gun,
Glanced just and sudden from the fowler's eye,
O'ertakes their sounding pinions, and again,
Immediate, brings them from the towering wing,
Dead to the ground, or drives them wide dispersed,
Wounded, and wheeling various, down the wind.

Thomson.

HARVEST.

And as the load jogg'd homeward down the lane,
When welcome night shut out the toiling day,
Following he mark'd the simple-hearted swain ;
Joying to listen, on his homeward way,
While rest's warm rapture roused the rustic's lay,
The threadbare ballad from each quavering tongue,
As "Peggy Band," or the "Sweet Month of May :"
Oh, how he joy'd to hear each "good old song,"
That on night's pausing ear did echo loud and long.

The muse might sing too ; for he well did know
The freaks and plays that harvest-labour end :
How the last load is crown'd with boughs, and how
The swains and maids with fork and rake attend,
With floating ribbons 'dizen'd at the end ;
And how the children on the load delight
With shouts of " Harvest home ! " their throats to rend ;
And how the dames peep out to mark the sight ;
And all the feats that crown the harvest-supper night.

Clare.

HARVEST SONG.

AUTUMN winds are sighing,
  Summer glories dying,
    Harvest-time is nigh.
Cooler breezes, quivering,
Through the pine-groves shivering,
  Sweep the troubled sky.

See the fields, how yellow!
Clusters, bright and mellow,
  Gleam on every hill;
Nectar fills the fountains,
Crowns the sunny mountains,
  Runs in every rill.

Now the lads are springing.
Maidens blithe are singing,
  Swells the harvest strain:
Every field rejoices;
Thousand thankful voices
  Mingle on the plain.

Then, when day declineth,
And the mild moon shineth,
  Tabours sweetly sound;
And, while they are sounding,
Fairy feet are bounding
  O'er the moonlit ground.
                Von Salis.

HARVEST SONG.

SICKLES sound : on the ground
Fast the ripe ears fall ;
Every maiden's bonnet has blue blossoms on it—
Joy is over all.

Sickles ring,
    Maidens sing
  To the sickle's sound ;
Till the moon is beaming,
And the stubble gleaming,
  Harvest songs go round.

All are springing,
    All are singing
  Every lisping thing ;
Man and master meat
From one dish they eat ;
  Each is now a king.

Hans and Michael
    Whet the sickle,
  Piping merrily.
Now they mow; each maiden
Soon with sheaves is laden,
  Busy as a bee !

Now the blisses,
    Now the kisses—
  Now the wit doth flow
Till the beer is out ;
Then with song and shout,
  Hence they go, yo ho !

Holty

SONNET.

THRICE happy he who by some shady grove,
    Far from the clamorous world, doth live his own ;
    Though solitary, who is not alone,
But doth converse with that Eternal Love.
Oh, how more sweet is bird's harmonious moan,
    Or the hoarse sobbings of the widow'd dove,
Than those smooth whisperings near a prince's throne,
    Which good make doubtful, do the ill approve !
Oh, how more sweet is zephyr's wholesome breath,
    And sighs embalm'd, which new-born flowers unfold,
Than that applause vain honour doth bequeath !
    How sweet are streams, to poisons drank in gold !
The world is full of horrors, troubles, slights ;
Woods' harmless shades have only true delights.

Drummond.

LITTLE STREAMS.

LITTLE streams are light and shadow,
Flowing through the pasture meadow
Flowing by the green wayside,
Through the forest dim and wide,
Through the hamlet still and small,
By the cottage, by the hall,
By the ruin'd abbey still,
Turning here and there a mill,
Bearing tribute to the river—
Little streams, I love you ever.

Summer music is there flowing—
Flowering plants in them are growing ;
Happy life is in them all,
Creatures innocent and small ;
Little birds come down to drink,
Fearless of their leafy brink ;
Noble trees beside them grow,
Glooming them with branches low ;
And between the sunshine glancing
In their little waves is dancing.

Little streams have flowers a many,
Beautiful and fair as any :
Typha strong, and green bur-reed,
Willow-herb, with cotton-seed ;
Arrow-head, with eye of jet,
And the water-violet.

There the flowering rush you meet,
And the plumy meadow-sweet ;

And in places deep and stilly,
Marble-like, the water-lily.

Little streams, their voices cheery,
Sound forth welcomes to the weary ;
Flowing on from day to day,
Without stint and without stay.
Here, upon their flowery bank,
In the old time pilgrims drank ;
Here have seen, as now, pass by,
King-fisher and dragon-fly,—
Those bright things that have their dwelling
Where the little streams are welling.

Down in valleys green and lowly,
Murmuring not and gliding slowly,
Up in mountain-hollows wild,
Fretting like a peevish child ;
Through the hamlet, where all day
In their waves the children play ;
Running west, or running east,
Doing good to man and beast—
Always giving, weary never,
Little streams, I love you ever.

Howitt.

THE RIVULETS.

Go up and mark the new-born rill,
   Just trickling from its mossy bed ;
Streaking the heath-clad hill
   With a bright emerald thread.

Canst thou her bold career foretell,
   What rocks she shall o'erleap or rend.

133

How far in ocean's swell
  Her freshening billows send ?

Perchance that little brook shall flow
  The bulwark of some mighty realm,
Bear navies to and fro,
  With monarchs at their helm.

Or canst thou guess how far away
  Some sister nymph, beside her urn,
Reclining night and day,
  'Mid reeds and mountain fern,

Nurses her store, with thine to blend,
  When many a moor and glen are past ;
Then in the wide sea end
  Their spotless lives at last ?

Even so the course of prayer who knows ?
  It springs in silence when it will—
Springs out of sight, and flows
  At first a lonely rill.

But streams shall meet it by and by,
  From thousand sympathetic hearts—
Together swelling high,
  Their chant of many parts.
      *   *   *   *

                          Keble.

THE WOODLAND SCENE.

NOR less attractive is the woodland scene,
Diversified with trees of every growth,

Alike, yet various.   Here the gay smooth trunks
Of ash, or lime, or beech, distinctly shine,
Within the twilight of their distant shades ;
There, lost behind a rising ground, the wood
Seems sunk, and shorten'd to its topmost boughs.
No tree in all the grove but has its charms,
Though each its hue peculiar ; paler some,
And of a wanish grey ; the willow such,
And poplar, that with silver lines its leaf,
And ash far stretching his umbrageous arm ;
Of deeper green the elm ; and deeper still,
Lord of the woods, the long-surviving oak.
Some glossy-leaved, and shining in the sun,
The maple, and the beech of oily nuts
Prolific, and the lime at dewy eve
Diffusing odours : nor unnoted pass
The sycamore, capricious in attire,
Now green, now tawny, and, ere autumn yet
Have changed the woods, in scarlet honours bright.

Cowper.

THE WAYSIDE SPRING.

AIR dweller by the dusty way,
  Bright saint within a mossy shrine,
The tribute of a heart to-day,
  Weary and worn, is thine.

The earliest blossoms of the year,
  The sweet-brier and the violet,
The pious hand of spring has here
  Upon thy altar set.

136

And not alone to thee is given
   The homage of the pilgrim's knee ;
But oft the sweetest birds of heaven
   Glide down and sing to thee.

Here daily from his beechen cell,
   The hermit squirrel steals to drink :

And flocks which cluster to their bell,
   Recline along thy brink.

And here the wagoner blocks his wheels,
   To quaff the cool and generous boon ;
Here from the sultry harvest-fields
   The reapers rest at noon.

And oft the beggar mask'd with tan,
   In rusty garments grey with dust,
Here sits and dips his little can,
   And breaks his scanty crust ;

And, lull'd beside thy whispering stream,
   Oft drops to slumber unawares,
And sees the angel of his dream
   Upon celestial stairs.

Dear dweller by the dusty way,
   Thou saint within a mossy shrine,
The tribute of a heart to-day,
   Weary and worn, is thine.   *Read.*

A GROVE.

HERE stood the elme, whose shade so mildly dim
Doth nourish all that groweth under him ;
Cipresse, that like piramids rune topping,
And hurt the least of any by their dropping ;
The alder, whose fat shadow nourisheth,
Each plant set neere to him long flourisheth ;
The heavy-headed plane-tree, by whose shade

The grasse grows thickest, men are fresher made ;
The oake, that best endures the thunder-shocks ;
The everlasting ebene, cedar, boxe ;
The olive that in wainscot never cleaves ;
The amorous vine which in the elme still weaves ;
The lotus, juniper, where worms ne'er enter ;
The pyne, with whom men through the ocean venter :
The war-like yeugh, by which (more than the lance)
The strong-arm'd English spirits conquer'd France.
Among the rest the tamariske there stoode,
For huswife's besoms only knowne most goode :
The cold-place-loving birch, and servis-tree ;
The walnut-loving vales, the mulberry ;
The maple, ashe, that doe delight in fountains,
Which have their currents by the side of mountains ;
The laurell, mirtle, ivy, date, which hold
Their leaves all winter, be it ne'er so cold ;
The firre, that oftentimes doth rosins drop ;
The beech, that scales the welkin with his top.
All these, and thousand more, within this grove,
By all the industry of nature strove
To frame an arbour that might keep within it,
The best of beauties that the world hath in it.

Browne.

SONG.

UNDER the greenwood tree
Who loves to lie with me,
And tune his merry note
Unto the sweet bird's throat,

Come hither, come hither, come hither;
  There shall he see
  No enemy,
But winter and rough weather.

  Who doth ambition shun
  And loves to live i' the sun,
  Seeking the food he eats,
  And pleased with what he gets,
Come hither, come hither, come hither;
  There shall he see
  No enemy,
But winter and rough weather.

        Shakspeare.

A WINTER SONG.

WHEN icicles hang by the wall,
   And Dick the shepherd blows his nail,
And Tom bears logs into the hall,
   And milk comes frozen home in pail;
When blood is nipp'd and ways be foul,
Then nightly sings the staring owl,
      To-whoo;
Tu-whit, to-whoo, a merry note,
While greasy Joan doth keel the pot.

When all aloud the wind doth blow,
   And coughing drowns the parson's saw,
And birds sit brooding in the snow,
   And Marian's nose looks red and raw ;
When roasted crabs hiss in the bowl,
Then nightly sings the staring owl,
         To-whoo ;
To-whit, to-whoo, a merry note,
While greasy Joan doth keel the pot.

                      Shakspeare.

A WINTER SCENE.

THE keener tempests rise ; and fuming dun,
From all the livid east, or piercing north,
Thick clouds ascend ; in whose capacious womb
A vapoury deluge lies, to snow congeal'd.
Heavy they roll their fleecy world along ;
And the sky saddens with the gather'd storm.
Through the hush'd air the whitening shower descends,
At first thin wavering ; till at last the flakes
Fall broad, and wide, and fast, dimming the sky,
With a continual flow. The cherish'd fields
Put on their winter robe of purest white.
'Tis brightness all ; save where the new snow melts
Along the mazy current. Low the woods
Bow their hoar head ; and, ere the languid sun,
Faint from the west, emits his evening ray,
Earth's universal face, deep hid and still,
Is one wild dazzling waste, that buries wide
The works of man. Drooping, the labourer-ox
Stands cover'd o'er with snow, and then demands
The fruit of all his toil. The fowls of heaven,

Tamed by the cruel season, crowd around
The winnowing store, and claim the little boon

Which Providence assigns them.   One alone,
The redbreast, sacred to the household gods,

Wisely regardful of th' embroiling sky,
In joyless fields and thorny thickets leaves
His shivering mates, and pays to trusted man
His annual visit.   Half afraid, he first
Against the window beats ; then, brisk, alights
On the warm hearth ; then, hopping o'er the floor,
Eyes all the smiling family askance,
And pecks, and starts, and wonders where he is :
Till, more familiar grown, the table crumbs
Attract his slender feet.   The foodless wilds
Pour forth their brown inhabitants.   The hare,
Though timorous of heart, and hard beset
By death in various forms, dark snares and dogs,
And more unpitying men, the garden seeks,
Urged on by fearless want.   The bleating kind
Eye the bleak heaven, and next the glistening earth,
With looks of dumb despair ; then, sad dispersed,
Dig for the wither'd herb through heaps of snow.

Thomson.

WINTER SONG.

UMMER joys are o'er ;
    Flow'rets bloom no more :
Wintry winds are sweeping ;
Through the snowdrifts peeping,
    Cheerful evergreen
    Rarely now is seen.

Now no plumèd throng
Charms the wood with song ;
Ice-bound trees are glittering ;

144

Merry snow-birds, twittering,
  Fondly strive to cheer
  Scenes so cold and drear.

  Winter, still I see
  Many charms in thee ;
Love thy chilly greeting,
Snow-storms fiercely beating,
  And the dear delights
  Of the long, long nights.   *Holty.*

WINTER.

THOU hast thy beauties : sterner ones, I own,
  Than those of thy precursors ; yet to thee
  Belong the charms of solemn majesty
And naked grandeur. Awful is the tone
  Of thy tempestuous nights, when clouds are blown
  By hurrying winds across the troubled sky ;
  Pensive, when softer breezes faintly sigh
Through leafless boughs,with ivy overgrown.
  Thou hast thy decorations too, although
  Thou art austere : thy studded mantle, gay
With icy brilliants, which as proudly glow
  As erst Golconda's ; and thy pure array
Of regal ermine, when the drifted snow
  Envelopes Nature ; till her features seem
  Like pale, but lovely ones, seen when we dream.
                               Barton.

WOODS IN WINTER.

WHEN winter winds are piercing chill,
 And through the hawthorn blows the gale,
With solemn feet I tread the hill
 That overbrows the lonely vale.

O'er the bare upland, and away
 Through the long reach of desert woods,
The embracing sunbeams chastely play,
 And gladden those deep solitudes

Where, twisted round the barren oak,
 The summer vine in beauty clung,
And summer winds the silence broke,
 The crystal icicle is hung ;

Where, from their frozen urns, mute springs
 Pour out the river's gradual tide,
Shrilly the skater's iron rings,
 And voices fill the woodland side.

Alas ! how changed from the fair scene,
 When birds sang out their mellow lay,
And winds were soft, and woods were green,
 And the song ceased not with the day.

But still wild music is abroad,
 Pale, desert woods ! within your crowd ;
And gathering winds in hoarse accord
 Amid the vocal reeds pipe loud.

Chill airs, and wintry winds! my ear
  Has grown familiar with your song;

I hear it in the opening year—
  I listen, and it cheers me long.   *Longfellow.*

SONNET.

HEATH'D is the river as it glideth by,
    Frost-pearl'd are all the boughs in forests
        old,
    The sheep are huddling close upon the
        wold,
    And over them the stars tremble on high.
    Pure joys, these winter nights, around
        me lie ;
    'Tis fine to loiter through the lighted
        streets
At Christmas time, and guess from brow and pace
The doom and history of each one we meet ;
What kind of heart beats in each dusky case ;
Whiles startled by the beauty of a face
In a shop-light a moment ; or, instead,
To dream of silent fields, where calm and deep
The sunshine lieth like a golden sleep—
Recalling sweetest looks of summers dead.

                        Smith.

NOVEMBER.

NOVEMBER'S sky is chill and drear ;
November's leaf is red and sere.
Late, gazing down the steepy linn
That hems our little garden in,
Low in its dark and narrow glen,
You scarce the rivulet might ken,

148

So thick the tangled green-wood grew,
So feeble trill'd the streamlet through :
Now murmuring hoarse, and frequent seen
Through bush and brier, no longer green,
An angry brook, it sweeps the glade,
Brawls over rock and wild cascade,
And, foaming brown with double speed,
Hurries its waters to the Tweed.

   No longer Autumn's glowing red
Upon our forest hills is shed ;
No more, beneath the evening's beam,
Fair Tweed reflects their purple gleam ;
Away hath pass'd the heather-bell
That bloom'd so rich on Needpath fell ;
Sallow his brow, and russet bare
Are now the sister-heights of Yare.
The sheep, before the pinching heaven,
To shelter'd dale and down are driven,
Where yet some faded herbage pines,
And yet a watery sunbeam shines ;
In meek despondency they eye
The wither'd sward and wintry sky,
And far beneath their summer hill,
Stray sadly by Glenkinnon's rill :
The shepherd shifts his mantle's fold,
And wraps him closer from the cold ;
His dogs no merry circles wheel,
But, shivering, follow at his heel ;
A cowering glance they often cast,
As deeper moans the gathering blast.

                             Scott.

WINTER.

ND in the frosty season, when the sun
    Was set, and visible for many a mile,
    The cottage-windows through the twilight blazed,
    I heeded not the summons : happy time
    It was indeed for all of us ; for me
    It was a time of rapture !   Clear and loud
    The village-clock toll'd six—I wheel'd about,
    Proud and exulting, like an untired horse
That cares not for his home.—All shod with steel
We hiss'd along the polish'd ice, in games
Confederate, imitative of the chase
And woodland pleasures,—the resounding horn,
The pack loud-chiming, and the hunted hare.
So through the darkness and the cold we flew,
And not a voice was idle : with the din
Smitten, the precipices rang aloud ;
The leafless trees and every icy crag
Tinkled like iron ; while the distant hills
Into the tumult sent an alien sound
Of melancholy, not unnoticed while the stars
Eastward, were sparkling clear, and in the west
The orange sky of evening died away.
    Not seldom from the uproar I retired
Into a silent bay, or sportively
Glanced sideways, leaving the tumultuous throng,
To cut across the reflex of a star ;
Image, that, flying still before me, gleamed
Upon the glassy plain : and oftentimes,
When we had given our bodies to the wind,

And all the shadowy banks on either side
Come sweeping through the darkness, spinning still

The rapid line of motion, then at once
Have I, reclining back upon my heels,

Stopp'd short ; yet still the solitary cliffs
Wheel'd by me—even as if the earth had roll'd
With visible motion her diurnal round !
Behind me did they stretch in solemn train,
Feebler and feebler, and I stood and watch'd
Till all was tranquil as a summer sea.

Wordsworth.

WINTER.

THIS is the eldest of the seasons : he
   Moves not like Spring, with gradual step, nor grows
   From bud to beauty, but with all his snows
Comes down at once in hoar antiquity.
No rains nor loud proclaiming tempests flee
   Before him, nor unto his time belong
   The suns of summer, nor the charms of song,
That with May's gentle smiles so well agree.
But he, made perfect in his birth-day cloud,
   Starts into sudden life with scarce a sound,
   And with a tender footstep prints the ground,
     As though to cheat man's ear : yet, while he stays,
     He seems as 'twere to prompt our merriest days,
And bid the dance and joke be long and loud.

Proctor.

COUNTRY-SPORTS

SONNET.

THERE is exhilaration in the chase—
 Not bodily only! Bursting from the woods,
Or having climbed some misty mountain's height,
 When on our eyes a glorious prospect opes,
With rapture we the golden view embrace:
 Then worshipping the sun on silver floods,
And blazing towers, and spires, and cities bright
 With his reflected beams; and down the slopes
The tumbling torrents; from the forest mass
 Of darkness issuing, we with double force
Along the gaily-checker'd landscape pass,
 And, bounding with delight, pursue our course.
It is a mingled rapture, and we find
The bodily spirit mounting to the mind.

Brydges.

ANCIENT HUNTING SONG.

HE hunt is up, the hunt is up!
Sing merrily we, the hunt is up:
    The birds they sing,
    The deer they fling,
    Hey, nonny, nony, no ;
    The hounds they cry,
    The hunters fly,
    Hey, trolilo, trololilo.
The hunt is up, the hunt is up!
Sing merrily we, the hunt is up!

    The wood resounds
    To hear the sounds,
    Hey, nonny, nony, no ;
    The rocks report
    This merry sport,
    Hey, trolilo, trololilo.
The hunt is up, the hunt is up!
Sing merrily we, the hunt is up!

    Then hie apace
    Unto the chase,
    Hey, nonny, nony, no !
    While every thing
    Doth sweetly sing
    Hey, trolilo, trololilo,
The hunt is up, the hunt is up!
Sing merrily we, the hunt is up!

Anon.

154

THE HUNT.

Hark! from yon covert, where those towering oaks
Above the humble copse aspiring rise,

155

What glorious triumphs burst in every gale
Upon our ravish'd ears ! The hunter's shout,
The clanging horns, swell their sweet-winding notes ;
The pack wide opening load the trembling air
With various melody ; from tree to tree
The propagated cry redoubling bounds,
And winged zepnyrs waft the floating joy
Through all tne regions near : afflictive birch
No more the schoolboy dreads ; his prison broke,
Scampering he flies, nor heeds his master's call ;
The weary traveller forgets his road,
And climbs th' adjacent hill : the ploughman leaves
Th' unfinish'd furrow ; nor his bleating flocks are now
The shepherd's joy ! Men, boys, and girls
Desert th' unpeopled village, and wild crowds
Spread o'er the plain, by the sweet frenzy seized.
Look, how she pants ! and o'er yon opening glade
Slips glancing by ! while, at the farther end,
The puzzled pack unravel wile by wile,
Maze within maze.

* * * * * * * *

But hold ! I see her from her covert break ;
Sad on yon little eminence she sits ;
Intent she listens, with one ear erect,
Pondering, and doubtful what new course to take,
And how t' escape the fierce, bloodthirsty crew
That still urge on, and still in valleys loud
Insult her woes, and mock her sore distress.
As now in louder peals the loaded winds
Bring on the gathering storm, her fears prevail,
And o'er the plain, and o'er the mountain's ridge,
Away she flies ; nor ships with wind and tide.
And all their canvas wings, scud half so fast
Once more, ye jovial train, your courage try,
And each clean courser's speed. We scour along,

In pleasing hurry and confusion lost !
Oblivion to be wished. The patient pack
Hang on the scent unwearied ; up they climb,
And ardent we pursue ; our labouring steeds
We press, we gore ; till once the summit gained,
Painfully panting, there we breathe awhile ;
Then, like a foaming torrent, pouring down
Precipitant, we smoke along the vale.
Happy the man who with unrivalled speed
Can pass his fellows, and with pleasure view
The struggling pack ; how in the rapid course
Alternate they preside, and jostling push
To guide the dubious scent ; how giddy youth,
Oft babbling, errs, by wiser age reproved ;
How niggard of his strength, the wise old hound
Hangs in the rear, till some important point
Rouse all his diligence, or till the chase
Sinking he finds : then to the head he springs,
With thirst of glory fired, and wins the prize,
* * * * * * * *
     And now in open view,
See, see, she flies ! each eager hound exerts
His utmost speed, and stretches every nerve.
How quick she turns ! their gaping jaws eludes,
And yet a moment lives ; till, round inclosed
By all the greedy pack, with infant screams
She yields her breath, and there reluctant dies !
         Somerville.

A HUNTER'S MATIN.

Up, comrades, up! the morn's awake
 Upon the mountain side,
The curlew's wing hath swept the lake,
And the deer has left the tangled brake,
 To drink from the limpid tide.

Up, comrades, up! the mead-lark's note
And the plover's cry o'er the prairie float;
The squirrel he springs from his covert now,
To prank it away on the chestnut bough,
Where the oriole's pendent nest, high up,
 Is rock'd on the swaying trees,
While the hum-bird sips from the harebell's cup,
 As it bends to the morning breeze.

Up, comrades, up! our shallops grate
 Upon the pebbly strand,
And our stalwart hounds impatient wait
 To spring from the huntsman's hand!

Hoffman.

NOVEMBER.

Hark through the greenwood ringing,
 Peels the merry horn;
 On, gallant steed,
 O'er dewy mead,
 Sir Asquetin is borne.

Many a brave and noble knight,
Pranceth proud on left and right.

With beagle good,
They draw the wood,
And loud and shrilly raise
The music of the chase,

159

Deep, deep within the forest,
Fast by fountain clear,
With dewdrop dank
Upon his flank,
Stands the noble deer.
See, he starts! for heard afar,
Come the notes of the woodland war;
And up he springs,
And on the wings
That mock the mountain wind,
Leaves hound and horn behind.

Sweet, sweet upon the mountain,
Sinks the setting sun;
The coursers fleet
Scarce drag their feet,
The weary chase is done,
But where's the antler'd king who late
Ranged his realms in fearless state?
Alas! alas!
Upon the grass
That his best heart's blood dyes,
The captured monarch lies.

Tytler.

THE TUNEFUL SOUND OF ROBIN'S HORN.

THE tuneful sound of Robin's horn
Hath welcomed thrice the blushing morn;
Then haste, Clorinda, haste away,
And let us meet the rising day.

And through the green-wood let us go,
With arrows keen, and bended bow ;
There breathe the mountain's fresh'ning gale,
Or scent the blossoms in the vale.

For nature now is in her prime,—
'Tis now the lusty summer time ;
When grass is green, and leaves are long,
And feather'd warblers tune their song.

At noon, in some sequester'd glade,
Beneath some oak-tree's ample shade,
We'll feast, nor envy all the fare
Which courtly dames and barons share.

See, see in yonder glen appear
In wanton herds the fallow deer ;
Then haste, my love, oh ! haste away,
And let us meet the rising day.

Anon.

WAKEN, LORDS AND LADIES GAY.

AKEN, lords and ladies gay,
On the mountain dawns the day,
All the jolly chase is here,
With horse, and hawk, and hunting spear !
Hounds are in their couples yelling,
Hawks are whistling, horns are knelling.
Merrily, merrily, mingle they,
" Waken, lords and ladies gay."

Waken, lords and ladies gay,
The mist has left the mountain grey,
Springless in the dawn are steaming,
Diamonds on the brake are gleaming,
And foresters have busy been,
To track the buck in thicket green ;
Now we come to chant our lay,
" Waken, lords and ladies gay."

Waken, lords and ladies gay,
To the green-wood haste away ;
We can show you where he lies,
Fleet of foot, and tall of size ;
We can show the marks he made,
When 'gainst the oak his antlers fray'd :
You shall see him brought to bay,
" Waken, lords and ladies gay."

Louder, louder chant the lay,
" Waken lords and ladies gay ;"
Tell them youth, and mirth, and glee,
Run a course as well as we ;
Time, stern huntsman, who can balk ?
Stanch as hound, and fleet as hawk ;
Think of this, and rise with day,
Gentle lords and ladies gay.

Scott.

AUTUMN.

N earliest hours of dark unhooded morn,
Ere yet one rosy cloud bespeaks the dawn,
Whilst far abroad the fox pursues his prey,
He's doom'd to risk the perils of the day,

162

From his stronghold block'd out ; perhaps to bleed,
Or owe his life to fortune. or to speed.
For now the pack, impatient rushing on,
Range through the darkest coverts one by one ;

Trace every spot ; whilst down each noble glade
That guides the eye beneath a changeful shade,
The loit'ring sportsman feels th' instinctive flame,
And checks his steed to mark the springing game.

Midst intersecting cuts and winding ways
The huntsman cheers his dogs, and anxious strays
Where every narrow riding, even shorn,
Gives back the echo of his mellow horn :
Till fresh and lightsome, every power untried,
The starting fugitive leaps by his side ;
His lifted finger to his ear he plies,
And the view halloo bids a chorus rise
Of dogs quick-mouth'd, and shouts that mingle loud,
As bursting thunder rolls from cloud to cloud.
With ears erect, and chest of vigorous mould,
O'er ditch, o'er fence, unconquerably bold,
The shining courser lengthens every bound,
And his strong footlocks suck the moisten'd ground,
As from the confines of the wood they pour,
And joyous villages partake the roar.
O'er heath far stretch'd, or down, or valley low,
The stiff-limb'd peasant, glorying in the show,
Pursues in vain ; where youth itself soon tires,
Spite of the transports that the chase inspires ;
For who unmounted long can charm the eye,
Or hear the music of the leading cry ?

Bloomfield.

ON CHRISTMAS.

WITH footstep slow, in furry pall yclad,
His brows enwreath'd with holly never sere,
Old Christmas comes, to close the wanèd year.
And aye the shepherd's heart to make right glad ;
Who, when his teeming flocks are homeward had,
To blazing hearth repairs, and nut-brown beer ;
And views, well pleased, the ruddy prattlers dear
Hug the grey mongrel ; meanwhile, maid and lad
Squabble for roasted crabs.   Thee, sire, we hail,
Whether thine aged limbs thou dost enshroud
In vest of snowy white and hoary veil,
Or wrapp'st thy visage in a sable cloud ;
Thee we proclaim with mirth and cheer, nor fail
To greet thee well with many a carol loud.

Bampfylde.

CHRISTMAS COMES BUT ONCE A YEAR.

THOSE Christmas bells as sweetly chime,
      As on the day when first they rung
So merrily in the olden time,
      And far and wide their music flung :
Shaking the tall grey ivied tower,
With all their deep melodious power :
      They still proclaim to every ear,
      Old Christmas comes but once a year.

Then he came singing through the woods,
      And pluck'd the holly bright and green ;
Pull'd here and there the ivy buds ;
      Was sometimes hidden, sometimes seen—
Half-buried 'neath the mistletoe,
His long beard hung with flakes of snow ;
      And still he ever caroll'd clear,
      Old Christmas comes but once a year.

He merrily came in days of old,
      When roads were few and ways were foul,
Now stagger'd, now some ditty troll'd,
      Now drank deep from his wassail bowl ;
His holly silver'd o'er with frost.
Nor never once his way he lost ;
      For, reeling here and reeling there,
      Old Christmas comes but once a year.

The hall was then with holly crown'd,
      'Twas on the wild-deer's antlers placed :
It hemm'd the batter'd armour round,
      And every ancient trophy graced.

166

It deck'd the boar's head, tusk'd and grim,
The wassail bowl wreath'd to the brim.

A summer-green hung everywhere,
For Christmas came but once a year.

His jaded steed the armèd knight
 Rein'd up before the abbey gate ;
By all assisted to alight,
 From humble monk to abbot great.
They placed his lance behind the door,
His armour on the rush-strewn floor ;
 And then brought out the best of cheer,
 For Christmas came but once a year.

The maiden then, in quaint attire,
 Loosed from her head the silken hood,
And danced before the yule-clog fire—
 The crackling monarch of the wood.
Helmet and shield flash'd back the blaze,
In lines of light, like summer rays,
 While music sounded loud and clear ;
 For Christmas came but once a year.

What though upon his hoary head
 Have fallen many a winter's snow ?
His wreath is still as green and red
 As 'twas a thousand years ago.
For what has he to do with care ?
His wassail bowl and old arm chair
 Are ever standing ready there,
 For Christmas comes but once a year.

No marvel Christmas lives so long,
 He never knew but merry hours,
His nights were spent with mirth and song,
 In happy homes and princely bowers ;
Was greeted both by serf and lord,
And seated at the festal board ;
 While every voice cried " Welcome here ! "
 Old Christmas comes but once a year.

But what care we for days of old,
　　The knights whose arms have turn'd to rust,
Their grim boars' heads, and pasties cold,
　　Their castles crumbled into dust?
Never did sweeter faces go,
Blushing beneath the mistletoe,
　　Than are to-night assembled here,
　　For Christmas still comes once a year.

For those old times are dead and gone,
　　And those who hail'd them pass'd away,
Yet still there lingers many a one,
　　To welcome in old Christmas Day.
The poor will many a care forget,
The debtor think not of his debt;
　　But, as they each enjoy their cheer,
　　Wish it was Christmas all the year.

And still around these good old times
　　We hang like friends full loth to part;
We listen to the simple rhymes
　　Which somehow sink into the heart.
" Half musical, half melancholy,"
Like childish smiles that still are holy,
　　A masquer's face dimm'd with a tear,
　　For Christmas comes but once a year.

The bells which usher in that morn
　　Have ever drawn my mind away
To Bethlehem, where Christ was born,
　　And the low stable where He lay,
In which the large-eyed oxen fed;
To Mary bowing low her head,
　　And looking down with love sincere,—
　　Such thoughts bring Christmas once a year.

At early day the youthful voice,
　　Heard singing on from door to door,
Makes the responding heart rejoice,
　　To know the children of the poor
For once are happy all day long ;
We smile and listen to the song,
　　The burthen still remote or near,
　　"Old Christmas comes but once a year."

Upon a gayer, happier scene
　　Never did holly-berries peer,
Or ivy throw its trailing green
　　On brighter forms than there are here ;
Nor Christmas in his old arm-chair
Smile upon lips and brows more fair :
　　Then let us sing amid our cheer,
　　"Old Christmas still comes once a year."　　*Miller.*

CHRISTMAS IN THE OLDEN TIME.

H EAP on more wood !—the wind is chill ;
But let it whistle as it will,
We'll keep our Christmas merry still.
Each age has deem'd the new-born year
The fittest time for festal cheer ;
And well our Christian sires of old
Loved when the year its course had roll'd,
And brought blithe Christmas back again,
With all his hospitable train.
Domestic and religious rite
Gave honour to the holy night :

On Christmas eve the bells were rung ;
On Christmas eve the mass was sung :

That only night, in all the year,
Saw the stoled priest the chalice rear.

The damsel donn'd her kirtle sheen ;
The hall was dress'd with holly green
Forth to the wood did merry men go,
To gather in the mistletoe ;
Then open'd wide the baron's hall
To vassal, tenant, serf, and all ;
Power laid his rod of rule aside,
And Ceremony doff'd his pride.
The heir, with roses in his shoes,
That night might village partner choose.
The lord, underogating, share
The vulgar game of " post and pair."
All hail'd, with uncontroll'd delight,
And general voice, the happy night,
That to the cottage, as the crown,
Brought tidings of salvation down.
The fire, with well-dried logs supplied,
Went roaring up the chimney wide ;
The huge hall-table's oaken face,
Scrubb'd till it shone, the day to grace,
Bore then upon its massive board
No mark to part the squire and lord.
Then was brought in the lusty brawn
By old blue-coated serving-man ;
Then the grim boar's head frown'd on high,
Crested with bays and rosemary.
Well can the green-garbed ranger tell,
How, when, and where the monster fell ;
What dogs before his death he tore,
And all the baiting of the boar.
The wassail round, in good brown bowls
Garnish'd with ribbons, blithely trowls.
There the huge sirloin reek'd ; hard by
Plum-porridge stood, and Christmas pie
Nor fail'd old Scotland to produce,
At such high tide, her savoury goose.

Then came the merry masquers in,
And carols roar'd with blithesome din ;
If unmelodious was the song,
It was a hearty note, and strong,—
Who lists may in their mumming see
Traces of ancient mystery.
White shirts supplied the masquerade,
And smutted cheeks the visors made ;
But, oh ! what masquers, richly dight,
Can boast of bosoms half so light !
England was merry England, when
Old Christmas brought his sports again.
'Twas Christmas broach'd the mightiest ale ;
'Twas Christmas told the merriest tale ;
A Christmas gambol oft could cheer
The poor man's heart through half the year.

Scott.

CHRISTMAS TIME.

GLAD Christmas comes, and every hearth
 Makes room to give him welcome now
E'en want will dry its tears in mirth,
 And crown him with a holly bough.
Though tramping 'neath a winter sky,
 O'er snowy paths and rimy stiles,
The housewife sets her spinning by,
 To bid him welcome with her smiles.

Each house is swept the day before,
 And windows stuck with evergreens ;
The snow is besomed from the door,
 And comfort crowns the cottage scenes.
Gilt holly with its thorny pricks,
 And yew, and box, with berries small,

These deck the unused candlesticks,
    And pictures hanging by the wall.

Neighbours resume their annual cheer,
    Wishing, with smiles and spirits high,
Glad Christmas and a happy year
    To every morning passer-by ; ·
Milkmaids their Christmas journeys go,
    Accompanied by a favour'd swain ;
And children pace the crumpling snow,
    To taste their granny's cake again.

The shepherd now no more afraid,
    Since custom doth the chance bestow,
Starts up to kiss the giggling maid
    Beneath the branch of mistletoe,
That 'neath each cottage beam is seen,
    With pearl-like berries shining gay ;
The shadow still of what hath been,
    Which fashion yearly fades away

The singing waits—a merry throng—
    At early morn, with simple skill,
Yet imitate the angel's song,
    And chaunt their Christmas ditty still ;
And, 'mid the storm that dies and swells
    By fits, in hummings softly steals
The music of the village bells,
    Ringing around their merry peals.

When this is past, a merry crew,
    Bedeck'd in masks and ribbons gay,
The Morris Dance their sports renew,
    And act their winter evening play.
The clown turn'd king, for penny praise,
    Storms with the actor's strut and swell,

And harlequin, a laugh to raise,
Wears his hunchback and tinkling bell.

And oft for pence and spicy ale,
With winter nosegays pinn'd before,

The wassail-singer tells her tale,
    And drawls her Christmas carols o'er.
While 'prentice boy, with ruddy face,
    And rime bepowder'd dancing locks,
From door to door, with happy face,
    Runs round to claim his " Christmas-box."

The block upon the fire is put,
    To sanction custom's old desires,
And many a fagot's bands are cut
    For the old farmer's Christmas fires ;
Where loud-tongued gladness joins the throng,
    And Winter meets the warmth of May,
Till, feeling soon the heat too strong,
    He rubs his shins and draws away.

While snows the window-panes bedim,
    The fire curls up a sunny charm,
Where, creaming o'er the pitcher's rim,
    The flowering ale is set to warm.
Mirth, full of joy as summer bees,
    Sits there its pleasures to impart,
And children, 'tween their parents' knees,
    Sing scraps of carols off by heart.

And some, to view the winter weathers,
    Climb up the window-seat with glee,
Likening the snow to falling feathers,
    In fancy's infant ecstasy ;
Laughing, with superstitious love,
    O'er visions wild that youth supplies,
Of people pulling geese above,
    And keeping Christmas in the skies.

As though the homestead trees were drest,
    In lieu of snow, with dancing leaves,

As though the sun-dried martin's nest,
 Instead of icicles, hung the eaves ;
The children hail the happy day—
 As if the snow were April's grass,
And pleased, as 'neath the warmth of May,
 Sport o'er the water froze to glass.

Thou day of happy sound and mirth,
 That long with childish memory stays,
How blest around the cottage hearth
 I met thee in my younger days,
Harping with rapture's dreaming joys
 On presents which thy coming found,
The welcome sight of little toys,
 The Christmas gift of cousins round !

About the glowing hearth at night,
 The harmless laugh and winter tale
Go round ; while parting friends delight
 To toast each other o'er their ale.
The cotter oft with quiet zeal
 Will, musing, o'er his Bible lean ;
While in the dark the lovers steal
 To kiss and toy behind the screen.

Old customs ! Oh ! I love the sound,
 However simple they may be ;
Whate'er with time hath sanction found
 Is welcome, and is dear to me.
Pride grows above simplicity,
 And spurns them from her haughty mind :
And soon the poet's song will be
 The only refuge they can find.
                                        Clare.

CHRISTMAS MINSTRELSY.

HE Minstrels play'd their Christmas tune
  To-night beneath my cottage eaves;
While, smitten by a lofty moon,
  The encircling laurels, thick with leaves,
Gave back a rich and dazzling sheen,
That overpower'd their natural green.

Through hill and valley every breeze
  Had sunk to rest with folded wings:
Keen was the air, but could not freeze,
  Nor check the music of the strings;
So stout and hardy were the band
That scraped the chords with strenuous hand!

And who but listened?—till was paid
  Respect to every inmate's claim:
The greeting given, the music play'd,
  In honour of each household name,
Duly pronounced with lusty call,
And "merry Christmas" wish'd to all!

O brother! I revere the choice
  That took thee from thy native hills;
And it is given thee to rejoice:
  Though public care full often tills
(Heaven only witness of the toil)
A barren and ungrateful soil.

Yet, would that Thou, with me and mine,
    Hadst heard this never-failing rite;
And seen on other faces shine
    A true revival of the light
Which Nature and these rustic powers,
In simple childhood, spread through ours!

For pleasure hath not ceased to wait
    On these expected annual rounds;
Whether the rich man's sumptuous gate
    Call forth the unelaborate sounds,
Or they are offer'd at the door
That guards the lowliest of the poor.

How touching, when, at midnight, sweep
    Snow-muffled winds, and all is dark,
To hear—and sink again to sleep!
    Or, at an earlier call, to mark,
By blazing fire, the still suspense
Of self-complacent innocence.

The mutual nod,—the grave disguise
    Of hearts with gladness brimming o'er;
And some unbidden tears that rise
    For names once heard, and heard no more;
Tears brighten'd by the serenade
For infant in the cradle laid.

Ah! not for emerald fields alone,
    With ambient streams more pure and bright
Than fabled Cytherea's zone
    Glittering before the Thunderer's sight,
Is to my heart of hearts endear'd
The ground where we were born and rear'd!

Hail, ancient Manners! sure defence,
    Where they survive, of wholesome laws ;
Remnants of love whose modest sense
    Thus into narrow room withdraws ;
Hail, Usages of pristine mould,
And ye that guard them, Mountains old !

Bear with me, Brother ! quench the thought
    That slights this passion, or condemns ;
If thee fond Fancy ever brought
    From the proud margin of the Thames,
And Lambeth's venerable towers,
To humbler streams and greener bowers.

Yes, they can make, who fail to find,
    Short leisure even in busiest days ;
Moments to cast a look behind,
    And profit by those kindly rays
That through the clouds do sometimes steal,
And all the far-off past reveal.

Hence, while the imperial City's din
    Beats frequent on thy satiate ear,
A pleased attention I may win
    To agitations less severe,
That neither overwhelm nor cloy,
But fill the hollow vale with joy !

                    Wordsworth.

EVENING.

SILENT and cool, now freshening breezes blow
Where groves of chestnut crown yon shadowy steep,
And all around the tears of evening weep
For closing day, whose vast orb, westering slow,
Flings o'er the embattled clouds a mellower glow ;
While pens of folded herds, and murmuring deep,
And falling rills, such gentle cadence keep,
As e'en might soothe the weary heart of woe.
Yet what to me is eve, what evening airs,
Or falling rills, or ocean's murmuring sound,
While sad and comfortless I seek in vain
Her who in absence turns my joy to cares,
And, as I cast my listless glances round,
Makes varied scenery but varied pain ?

Camoens.

PROGRESS OF EVENING.

ROM yonder wood mark blue-eyed Eve proceed :
   First through the deep, and warm, and secret
      glens,
   Through the pale-glimmering, privet-scented
      lane,
   And through those alders by the river-side :
   Now the soft dust impedes her, which the sheep
   Have hollow'd out beneath their hawthorn
      shade.
   But ah ! look yonder ! see a misty tide
   Rise up the hill, lay low the frowning grove,
Enwrap the gay, white mansion, sap its sides,
Until they sink and melt away like chalk.
Now it comes down against our village tower,
Covers its base, floats o'er its arches, tears
The clinging ivy from the battlements—
Mingles in broad embrace the obdurate stone—
All one vast ocean ! and goes swelling on,
Slow and silent, dim and deepening waves.

                Landor.

NIGHT SONG.

THE moon is up in splendour,
And golden stars attend her ;
  The heavens are calm and bright ;
Trees cast a deepening shadow,
And slowly off the meadow
  A mist is rising silver-white.

Night's curtains now are closing
Round half a world reposing
In calm and holy trust :

All seems one vast, still chamber,
Where weary hearts remember
No more the sorrows of the dust.   *Claudius.*

183

MOONLIGHT NIGHT.

'TIS midnight ; on the mountains brown
The cold round Moon shines deeply
down ;
Blue roll the waters, blue the sky
Spreads like an ocean hung on high,
Bespangled with those isles of light,
So wildly, spiritually bright ;
Who ever gazed upon them shining,
And turn'd to earth without repining,
Nor wish'd for wings to flee away,
And mix with their eternal ray ?

Byron.

MOONLIGHT NIGHT.

HOW beautiful is Night !
A dewy freshness fills the silent air ;
No mist obscures, nor cloud, nor speck, nor stain,
Breaks the serene of heaven :
In full-orb'd glory yonder Moon divine
Rolls through the dark-blue depths.
Beneath her steady ray
The desert circle spreads,
Like the round Ocean, girdled with the sky.
How beautiful is Night !

Southey.

TO CYNTHIA.

QUEEN and huntress, chaste and fair,
  Now the sun is laid to sleep ;
Seated in thy silver chair,
  State in wonted manner keep :
Hesperus entreats thy light,
Goddess excellently bright !

Earth, let not thy envious shade
  Dare itself to interpose ;
Cynthia's shining orb was made
  Heaven to clear when day did close ;
Bless us, then, with wishèd sight,
Goddess excellently bright !

Lay thy bow of pearl apart,
  And thy crystal-shining quiver ;
Give unto the flying hart
  Space to breathe, how short soever ;
Thou that mak'st a day of night,
Goddess excellently bright !

Ben Jonson.

EVENING.

'ER the heath the heifer strays
  Free ;—(the furrow'd task is done)—
Now the village windows blaze,
  Burnish'd by the setting sun.

Now he sets behind the hill,
   Sinking from a golden sky ;
Can the pencil's mimic skill
   Copy the refulgent dye ?

Trudging as the ploughmen go
   (To the smoking hamlet bound),
Giant-like their shadows grow,
   Lengthening o'er the level ground.

Where the rising forest spreads
   Shelter for the lordly dome,
To their high-built airy beds
   See the rooks returning home.

As the lark with varied tune
   Carols to the evening loud,
Mark the mild resplendent moon
   Breaking through a parted cloud !

Now the hermit owlet peeps
   From the barn or twisted brake,
And the blue mist slowly creeps,
   Curling on the silent lake.

As the trout, in speckled pride,
   Playful from its bosom springs,
To the banks a ruffled tide
   Verges in successive rings.

Tripping through the silken grass,
O'er the path-divided dale,

Mark the rose-complexion'd lass
With her well-poised milking-pail.

Linnets with unnumber'd notes,
  And the cuckoo bird with two,
Tuning sweet their mellow throats,
  Bid the setting sun adieu.

                 Cunningham.

MOONLIGHT NIGHT.

OW beautiful this Night! The balmiest sigh
  Which vernal zephyrs breathe in Evening's
    ear,
Were discord to the speaking quietude
That wraps this moveless scene. Heaven's
  ebon vault,
Studded with stars unutterably bright,
Through which the Moon's unclouded
  grandeur rolls,
Seems like a canopy which Love had
  spread
To curtain her sleeping world. Yon
  gentle hills;
Robed in a garment of untrodden snow ;
Yon darksome walls, whence icicles depend,
So stainless that their white and glittering spears
Tinge not the Moon's pure beam ; yon castled steep,
Whose banner hangeth o'er the time-worn tower
So idly, that wrapt Fancy deemeth it
A metaphor of Peace,—all form a scene
Where musing Solitude might love to lift
Her soul above this sphere of earthliness ;

Where Silence undisturb'd might watch alone,
So cold, so bright, so still.   *Shelley.*

NIGHT.

IGHT, dew-lipp'd, comes, and every gleaming star
   Its silent place assigns in yonder sky ;
The moon walks forth, and fields and groves
   afar,
   Touch'd by her light, in silver beauty lie
In solemn peace, that no sound comes to mar ;
   Hamlets and peopled cities slumber nigh ;
While on this rock, in meditation's mien,
Lord of the unconscious world, I sit unseen.

How deep the quiet of this pensive hour !
   Nature bids labour cease—and all obey.
How sweet this stillness, in its magic power
   O'er hearts that know her voice and own
      her sway !
Stillness unbroken, save when from the flower
   The whirling locust takes his upward way ;
And, murmuring o'er the verdant turf, is heard
The passing brook—or leaf by breezes stirr'd.

Borne on the pinions of Night's freshening air,
   Unfetter'd thoughts with calm reflection come ;
And fancy's train, that shuns the daylight glare,
   To wake when midnight shrouds the heavens in gloom :
Now tranquil joys, and hopes untouch'd by care,
   Within my bosom throng to seek a home ;
While far around the brooding darkness spreads,
And o'er the soul its pleasing sadness sheds.

                                    Findemonte.

NIGHT.

IGHT is the time for rest ;
　　How sweet, when labours close,
　To gather round an aching breast
　　The curtain of repose,
Stretch the tired limbs, and lay the head
Down on our own delightful bed !

　Night is the time for dreams ;
　　The gay romance of life,
When truth that is, and truth that seems,
　　Mix in fantastic strife :
Ah ! visions, less beguiling far
Than waking dreams by daylight are.

Night is the time for toil ;
　　To plough the classic field,
Intent to find the buried spoil
　　Its wealthy furrows yield ;
Till all is ours that sages taught,
That poets sang and heroes wrought.

Night is the time to·weep ;
　　To wet with unseen tears
Those graves of memory where sleep
　　The joys of other years ;
Hopes that were angels at their birth,
But died when young, like things of earth.

Night is the time to watch ;
　　O'er ocean's dark expanse,
To hail the Pleiades, or catch

The full moon's earliest glance,
That brings into the home-sick mind
All we have loved and left behind.

Night is the time for care,
  Brooding on hours mis-spent,
To see the spectre of Despair,
  Come to our lonely tent;
Like Brutus, 'midst his slumbering host,
Summon'd to die by Cæsar's ghost.

Night is the time to think;
  When, from the eye, the soul
Takes flight, and, on the utmost brink
  Of yonder starry pole,
Discerns beyond the abyss of night
The dawn of uncreated light.

Night is the time to pray:
  Our Saviour oft withdrew
To desert mountains far away;
  So will His followers do,—
Steal from the throng to haunts untrod,
And commune there alone with God.

Night is the time for death;
  When all around is peace,
Calmly to yield the weary breath,
  From sin and suffering cease,
Think of heaven's bliss, and give the sign
To parting friends;—such death be mine.

Montgomery.

LONDON: R. CLAY, SONS, AND TAYLOR, PRINTERS.

www.ingramcontent.com/pod-product-compliance
Lightning Source LLC
Chambersburg PA
CBHW030547040726
47497CB00008B/2613